Off Center In The Attic

Off Center In The Attic

Over the Top Stories

Mary Deal

Titles by Mary Deal

Fiction
The Ka, a paranormal Egyptian suspense
River Bones, the original Sara Mason Mystery
The Howling Cliffs, 1st sequel to River Bones
Legacy of the Tropics, adventure/suspense
Down to The Needle, a thriller

Collections
Off Center in the Attic – Over the Top Stories

Nonfiction
Write It Right – Tips for Authors – The Big Book
Hypno-Scripts: Life-Changing Techniques Using Self-Hypnosis
and Meditation

What You'll Find in this Book

The flash story, **The Last Thing I Do**, appeared in *Freckles to Wrinkles*, an anthology by Silver Boomer Books, who also nominated it for the coveted **Pushcart Prize**.

Humor and nonsense, flights of fantasy into other realms, fright, disgust and disappointment, silliness and wonderment, and the sadness of reality and heartache. It's all here and more in stories that may leave you a little *Off Center in the Attic*, conjured through a mind that may be a little *Off Center in the Attic*.

Contents

Acting in a Coffin

Constance Faring was the most dynamic actress to make the Hollywood scene in decades. Her old-fashioned name alone suggested a lot of class and she had it all, including long, straight glistening brunette tresses. When it came to acting, she was not only blessed with a sense of humor but could play anyone from regal matriarch to prostitute.

Then along came Arlo Denny, a new breed of director, who angered Hollywood's elite while trampling his way to the top. He insisted on being referred to as *The Denny*. Underneath the personality façade, he was something of a wimp with a passion for playing cruel jokes to compensate. Although new to film directing, his first major effort became a mega-hit and garnered him an Oscar. Too sure of himself, his joking oftentimes lurched way out of control. He was on a roll and thought his sense of humor untouchable.

The Denny cast Constance in a short role of a woman who gets killed off. While Constance had proven she could play a variety of roles, she wasn't fond dying off early. The story was based around a funeral. Constance disliked the plot from the beginning but it was three months before her next film would begin shooting. Her agent suggested she take the part in Denny's film to have her name associated with this hot Hollywood mogul. It would take only six weeks to shoot.

"And by the way," her agent said. "Watch out for a guy named Barnard who works on Denny's crew. The two of them together could ignite."

So Constance's character died off, but Constance didn't disappear from the set. In fact, she had to lie perfectly still in the coffin for the duration of most of the rest of the scenes. That meant filming an endless number of scenes and angles as other actors and actresses played out their parts. Most of the film was to be shot around her lying in the coffin.

Part of the wimp director's repertoire of sic humor was playing jokes on set. Of course, where else? Everyone talked about retribution, but heaven forbid if someone out-did his antics. What kind of get even pranks might the demented director pull while trying to best everyone?

Barnard was a cameraman and insisted his name be pronounced *Ber-nerd,* plus he thought The Denny was way cool. Barnard had a dry sense of humor and tried to emulate The Denny. Unlike The Denny, who would laugh and dance around after pulling off some shenanigans, Barnard could pull off a joke with the straightest of faces and never so much as smile when people finally caught on. He might have been the best actor on the lot.

Filming a night scene called for the coffin lid being closed. No problem with Constance. In acting, she would rise to the cause for the sake of the film. After making sure she would be okay in a closed coffin—Constance joked that she would catch a catnap—down came the set lights and down came the cushioned lid close to her nose.

Constance could hear and understand the action happening on the set. While making changes and repositioning people and generally not being able to make up his mind, The Denny called a lunch break. He convinced everyone not to tell Constance for a while, but she had heard. Who knew that sound could reach the inside of a closed coffin? The dead never told.

"You coming?" a voice yelled from across the set. It was the voice of Gina Greg, the producer.

"I'll be right there." The Denny's voice sounded close by where Constance lay.

Someone snapped one of the hinges on the coffin lid. She wouldn't be able to get out! She heard The Denny chuckling to himself and imagined him slinking away.

Constance knew what The Denny had done and why. She wasn't dead. She listened as people left the set. Lunch would be only half an hour, less if everyone wolfed the fare from the lunch wagon before it hit their taste buds. As she lay in total darkness, she realized that idiot comedian of a director meant to leave her there through the entire lunch period. Well, she was would give him a surprise.

Feeling around in the dark, she rubbed her eyes with her fingertips to smear the heavy eye shadow and mascara together. She hoped her eyes would look like two blackened holes. With layers of powder on her skin to make her look pallid, her eyes would look sunken, empty, and ghoulish. She rubbed some of the dark mascara across her two front teeth to hide them. She smeared her painted lips larger than actual size and dribbled some down the corner of her mouth hoping to make it look like oozing blood. She managed to get her hands up behind her head and took down her fancy hairdo and draped some locks over her face. Then for one final touch.

She touched her fingertips in the lipstick and scraped them down the white satin inside the coffin lid hoping the marks would look like blood, as if she tried to claw her way out of the coffin. Anyone seeing her in the dimmed lights of the night scene might think she had been buried alive.

Soon, excited and accusatory voices burst onto the set.

"It was your idea to break suddenly for lunch," Gina was saying. "You open the coffin."

"I can't," The Denny said. "If something's happened to her, I won't be able to live with myself." He didn't sound that convincing.

"Open it now," another person said.

"She said she'd take a nap," The Denny said.

"No one naps in a coffin."

"If anything's happened to her, it'll ruin the shoot. Get the cameras on this. I want this all documented."

"Just open the damned thing!"

Constance heard the cameras being rolled across the set. Bernard would zoom in for a great close-up. She was prepared to make a scene they probably wouldn't expect from her.

Slowly, the lid began to open. Constance didn't wait. She threw back the lid and sat up fast and was right up in The Denny's face. She lunged for his neck and gurgled like a vampire about to suck a blood meal.

Everyone jumped backwards. Gina understood the joke and she and everyone else began to howl.

The Denny fainted.

Constance smiled a ghoulish grin and bounded out, white lace and fluff, to the floor.

Barnard and several of the crew picked up the unconscious director and placed him into the coffin. Bernard's smile was devious.

Just as Constance walked away with the makeup artist, she heard a familiar click of one of the latches on the coffin.

Everyone laughed and joked and waited out the half hour of retribution. From inside the coffin, The Denny must have regained consciousness. He wailed and kicked ferociously, as if taking a turn at acting out a part in a horror film. Finally, he quieted. He must have known they'd make him wait just as long.

After the half hour break, Barnard went to open the coffin as everyone watched. When he opened the lid, the inside of the coffin had been torn to shreds. The Denny did not spring out like Constance did. He didn't even move.

Barnard seemed stunned. Was he trying to prove his acting ability again? He bent down with an ear toward The Denny's face, straightened quickly and looked frightened. He put two fingers to The Denny's throat and waited and finally looked around, wide-eyed. "Oh, gad!" he said. "He's dead!"

The Wallflower

My two mannerly friends and I sit at our table and watch you walk into the room. People notice you, especially the guys. Your clothes are eye-catching and a bit more daring than I would think of wearing, but I don't accept every style change that comes along. Maybe that's why I occasionally feel like a wallflower in last month's trends. Your patent red stilettos draw attention to the fact that you've learned to walk on tiptoes. At least doing so is said to keep the calf muscles firm.

That tight black mini skirt could easily show the meeting place of your legs but it does make you appear smaller than you are. The plunging neckline of your beaded and sequined red silk blouse exemplifies the fact that you carry some weight, most of it above your waistband, and that acts as if it would rather break out and roam free. Your bangles and beads jingle and sparkle as only costume jewelry can. Could the glitz of your bling be why no one comments on the diamond tennis bracelet and other jewelry I patiently paid off over time in order to have pieces of value that will last? The sparkle of mine is subtle and pure under the lights of the nearby dance floor, but my jewelry doesn't make noise.

You find your table but don't sit to give the guys a chance to notice you. That's our way, but much too slow for you, the ultimate woman of the moment. My friends and I know your moves too well and watch you play them out as we smile in disbelief behind our table napkins.

You fling your tiny red evening bag into a chair and begin swiveling your way around the room talking to every guy along the way and flipping your tinted hair using provocative gestures and batting false eyelashes. Your cleavage bounces and rolls as you gyrate your way from table to table. Some of the guys reach for you, as if they want you to stay with them a little longer. Some follow and join you in others' conversations as if trying to claim you.

Other women in the room seem intimidated and drag their guys to the dance floor when you get a little too close to their tables. I'll bet I'm not the only person who expects you to break into song like a speak-easy entertainer of old who parks herself on the edge of some guy's table, or in his lap. Your voice and laughter have a way of quieting a room and drawing attention. Unlike you, too much noise and attention to me and my face turns red.

You pass our table and look at my friends and me only momentarily so you don't have to read our expressions. You know we understand what's happening here. You pucker up thick glossy red lips and move on. Or is that a fake pucker from the injections you've had to enlarge the thin upper lip you had a few months ago? Your colorful eye makeup would make Nefertiti envious but, surely, her perfume was more subtle. The red blush under your cheek bones accentuates both your jaw line and your fish-like pout.

Strange, too, is how once you spend an hour or so making your way around the room, you manage to corner some of the most eligible guys into a group and fawn over them, or they over you. As the night goes on you have trouble holding your glass upright. Strange, too, is how the guy you seem to favor begs out of the conversation leaving you with the others, even though you reach for him and try to draw him back.

Disbelief is your expression when he turns and walks straight over to our table and asks me to dance. As we whirl past you, the look you see on my face is not an expression of gloating. It's simply the naturally blushing wallflower being thankful for being real. But I can't help wonder who you really are and what you're hiding behind the façade you've felt the need to build around yourself.

Pupule

Moke Manoa was a little nuts. At least, that's what the neighbors told Kamaki and Lina Akamu when they moved next door to the scrawny, elderly Hawaiian. The neighbors called the strange man *Pupule*, saying his brain was split in half. Pupule. Crazy. He always wore the same clothes and talked to himself and walked a little stooped over. Rain or shine, he rode a rusting three-wheeled adult tricycle with a basket on the rear loaded with bags of who-knew-what. A tiny flag waved high on a pole attached to the back of his seat so people could see him in traffic. The neighbors said Moke used to own a lot of farm acreage but got too old to take care of it. He sold it off and bought the plantation house he now lived in and saved the rest of the money to carry him through old age. He was Portuguese-Hawaiian on his father's side and Filipino-Chinese on his mother's; a mixture from preceding generations, like many Hawaiians; like Kamaki and Lina, a slender, mixed-Asian looking couple with graying hair.

Some days Kamaki might say, "Lina, you come go see! He's doin' it again." They would watch the pupule through his kitchen window. Some days he danced and sang having fun. Other times, he angrily beat his metal dipping ladle and other utensils on the table and talked gibberish in pigeon English loud enough for the whole neighborhood to hear.

The days he started talking nonsense meant soon he would be out in the back yard. He had a habit of throwing some smelly stuff into the corner of his yard, farthest away from the house. The tropical heat rotted it and the bugs finished it off, and it left a stink hole where nothing grew. The trade winds being what they were on the northern-most Hawaiian Island of Kauai, Lina and Kamaki were unfortunate because the house in which they planned to spend the rest of their lives sat downwind from the stench. Even their friends avoided coming over. The neighbors seemed cruel and wanted nothing to do with Pupule. They had given up on trying to make him stop making that smell. At least when Lina and Kamaki saw him dance happily, they knew he would not be dumping a pot load that day.

As time went by, they decided to ask the pupule not to make that stench in his yard. It forced them to abandon their lovely patio and to crank the window jalousies tightly closed to try to keep the smell out of the house.

Kamaki and Lina were usually quiet and patient. Now they needed to tactfully speak out, and soon. Lina thought it would be wise to let the talk be man to man. When they had a chance to speak to Moke, Lina nudged her husband.

"Cuz," Kamaki said, using the island term that meant friendship. "Why you throw soup in back yard. No like?"

"*Pilau!*" Moke said. "Spoil."

What could that pupule have in his house that would force him to continually throw out big boiling pots of stuff under his back-yard bushes? On trash pickup day, his three big garbage cans reeked the same way. Lina and Kamaki had wondered why the price on the newer house they bought for retirement in the serene Wailua Homesteads sold so cheap. Now that they were settled in for a few months, they knew. The gossiping neighbors said the real estate broker must have paid Pupule not to dump till someone bought the house next door.

"What's worse?" Kamaki would scratch his head and ask. "Hearing chickens squawking at other house… or *pilapilau* next door?"

The Akamus were the only ones to occasionally speak to Pupule. Since they were newest to the neighborhood, the neighbors decided to leave it to them to put an end to the stink.

When Lina and Kamaki built up their nerve to approach the pupule once more, they were suddenly haltered in their tracks. Moke burst out the back door of his house, mumbling all the way to the far bushes where he sent the yellowish contents of another pot sailing through the air. Turning back, he mumbled loudly, not noticing them as they tried to get his attention through the Plumeria trees in their side yard.

The Akamus came up with another approach. They figured since Moke was elderly and living alone they should take him some food. They shopped the farmer's market in Old Town Kapaa and bought a selection of vegetables. With those, he could make a hearty stir-fry. Finally, they knocked at his door.

Moke opened the door and turned back into his house, muttering again. Present was that mild odor again, one that threatened to go bad. His gibberish didn't sound too confused so they decided to enter. In spite of the unkempt weeds around the house, they were surprised to see Moke's tiny single-wall island home spotlessly neat and clean inside. They found him in the kitchen stirring a huge pot of something, but the kitchen was a mess. They offered their vegetables and emptied out the bags on the table so Moke could see what they brought for him. He just stood smiling at them, looked at the vegetables and back to them again. Finally, Moke picked up a big Maui onion, squeezed it and put it down. He picked up some turnips, felt them cautiously and put them down.

"You like?" Moke asked. "Moke make?"

"For you, Cuz," Kamaki said.

"No, you bring," he said, holding up the turnips. "Many more." He cupped both hands to show how many more he wanted. Surely, he liked turnips. He turned back to the stove and ignored them. They tried to get his attention and he only motioned to the turnips and said, *"Nui 'ino."* Soon he began to mumble again and count on his fingers.

Getting through to a pupule was going to take some doing. The next week they went again to the farmers market and bought a whole bunch of turnips. Moke was not home so they left them in Lina's blue shopping bag on Moke's lanai beside the front door. Two days later, the blue bag showed up at their front door containing several small jars of canned food in yellow brine. They had the pupule's smell on them. Lina and Kamaki hesitated but took them inside and sat down at the kitchen table to examine them.

Finally, Lina said, "Brave husband, try one."

Once the lid was off the jar, out wafted a most delicate odor they never thought could come from something connected to a pupule. The scent was tantalizing. Kamaki pinched out a piece and bit into it. As he chewed slowly, he continued to say, "Um-m...umm!"

Lina knew from the look on his face that he had just had a taste of heaven. She begged for a bite and Kamaki held a wedge to her mouth. She bit into it and chewed slowly and swallowed. "'*Ono loa*!" she said. "Such delicious flavor."

Turnips. They were turnips, the ones they had purchased for Moke. They ate more. It was not dinnertime but they brought other foods out of the fridge and ate a small meal. Those pickled turnips enhanced the other foods.

"That's why he want more," Lina said. "He want make for us."

"We no see him cook again," Kamaki said. "But he cook *ono*."

"Then why throw other times in back yard?"

"Maybe he no can eat all." Kamaki ate another piece. The little jar was almost empty.

"But no have to cook to pickle, only leave sit in brine to cure." Lina shrugged and ate the last bite of her turnip wedge.

"Wonder what makes him *huhu* to mumble to himself and beat on table."

It was puzzling. They had to know more about this neighbor whom the other neighbors thought had a split brain but knew how to pickle turnips.

"Why you no save?" Kamaki asked the next time he saw Moke throwing something out. "Why spoil?"

Moke only smiled doubtfully and went back into his house. Lina and Kamaki decided to go over and see what they could do to help Moke avoid such waste. In Moke's kitchen, they watched him try to remember something. He would repeat several words, lose his train of thought and start over. Then Lina figured out that he was trying to remember some ingredients. "You try memorize cookbook?" she asked.

Moke had cookbooks haphazardly cast aside. He picked up one. "No good," he said. "Brine too strong." He tapped his chest. "My brine good. Make my brine."

"You cook brine to pickle vegetables?" Lina asked, surprised. She had just learned something from this pupule.

"My recipe... my recipe," he said. He flagged a hand toward several other cookbooks. "No good."

In his strange way, Moke was telling them that he had developed his own recipe for pickling. Lina and Kamaki finally understood and smiled at each other. Moke had been throwing out his brine if it did not turn out after he cooked it. Throwing it out in the back yard and making that stench.

"Why you no use garbage disposal?" Kamaki asked.

"No got."

"Why you throw in back yard?"

"Same as farm in country," he said. "Throw in field." So that was how his habit of throwing the brine into the back yard got started.

"You need to use the sink, Bro," Kamaki said, nicely using another familiar local term.

"No got grinding machine," he said.

Now that they knew for sure, they could not be upset with the man. He was elderly and a little pupule but doing something he loved to do.

"Why you pickle? You no eat regular food?"

Again, Moke only smiled. Up close, though his teeth were ugly with stains, he still had them all. He opened the fridge. Inside sat containers most likely filled with leftovers or cut vegetables ready to cook. He had plenty of food and the containers were stacked neatly. He was eating well.

"Why you pickle?" Kamaki asked again.

"Income," Moke said.

"Income? You sell?"

"Maybe tomorrow." That meant he was not ready to sell or, perhaps, he had not perfected his creation. He looked frustrated with himself.

"Where's recipe?" Lina asked.

"No got." He stirred the pot and did not look up.

"You no use recipe?"

He looked a little sheepish and feebly pointed to his head.

"You memorize it?" Kamaki asked. "He makes recipe as he goes," he said to Lina. "That's why he throws in yard. Sometimes doesn't make good."

Moke danced in his youngish feeble way. "Yeah!" he said, swinging his arms. "Yeah!"

They were finally getting somewhere. "You write ingredients and measures?" Lina asked.

Moke probably did not and could not remember correctly and that was why some days he threw out and some days danced happily instead. "No time," he said.

She studied him and his half-smile showed a little embarrassment. She could not believe what she was thinking. Moke did not know how to write. He only read enough to partially understand a cookbook. That was why he thought he had a better recipe. But he did have a better recipe. They had eaten his *ono* product and wanted more.

A few days later, they peeped cautiously through their window as a morning rain shower let up. Moke was getting ready to cook again. They rushed over with pen and paper. As he worked with ingredients, Lina did her best to understand his crude way of measuring ingredients and wrote it all down. That batch did not turn out. Kamaki helped Pupule throw out the brine in the yard!

Lina had tasted the brine and knew where to make the adjustments. They tried again the next day and surprisingly got it right.

"Ah-h-h, now make sale," Moke said. "Make retirement!" He took their hands and playfully swung their arms like children until he got tears in his eyes and left the room.

That one statement and him leaving the room told them so much. From other rumors they had heard, they guessed that Moke had outlived his retirement savings. He was trying desperately in his loneliness to create something that would bring him a little income in addition to his meager Social Security check. He probably had no dental insurance and that was why his teeth were so dark. Who knew what else he suffered without?

Kamaki did not waste time. He and Lina took two one-pint jars of turnips and contacted Aka, a friend and cook at a local tourist hotel along the Coconut Coast. When Aka tasted a wedge, he quickly finished it off and reached for another.

"You like, you buy," Kamaki said.

Lina stood silent beside her husband but from her angle, could see into the kitchen and there stood one of their neighbors, the one who gossiped the worst about Moke. Lina motioned to Aka. "You give other man in kitchen. He try."

Aka thought that was a great idea. He carried both jars back to the other cook. A little later he returned with a smile showing all teeth. One jar was empty and he handed it back. "Other cook keep," he said, referring to the second jar. "He like take home to wife. He say, 'Ono turnip!'"

Lina peeked again and saw the other cook finishing off a turnip wedge. By the look on his face, he loved it. Their busybody neighbor loved Moke's pickled turnips!

Moke could be the most misunderstood person they knew. Lina was tired of hearing the neighbors talking poorly about him. Their derogatory conversations focused on others as well and it wasn't fair to anyone. People needed to practice patience and tolerance with one another. In her mind, on a larger scale, lack of the two qualities was why the world was in such a sad state. If understanding began at home, the people of her neighborhood were about to get a good lesson.

"You no sell anywhere else," Aka said. It was a statement, not a question.

"I going sell everywhere," Kamaki said.

"No, you no sell, only here," Aka said. "More customer come this hotel, eat pickled vegetable."

Kamaki pulled his chin back like he was bracing himself. "Why you no tell bread man no sell anywhere else?"

"Huh?" Aka said. "All tourist eat bread, all hotels."

"Okay," Kamaki said. "So all tourist need eat pickled vegetable too."

"No sell anywhere else," Aka said again. "Make too much competition for business."

Kamaki and Lina smiled at one another. Lina knew her husband was about to give Aka a much-needed lesson in remembering the meaning of aloha.

"Okay," Kamaki said finally. "No sell other hotels... one month. But friend needs make income. You sell plenty. Help old Island boy."

"Only one month? I want be first sell," Aka said. He thought a moment and asked, "Old Island boy? How old this Island boy?"

"One *kahiʻko kanaka* on Social Security," Kamaki said.

"Oh, that kine old Island boy," he said. He finally understood. His expression softened.

"Only one month," Kamaki said. "You order one month supply, pay in advance, if you want sell only."

Aka nodded, knowing he needed to help a fellow Islander. "You bring fresh every week," he said. "I help old *kanaka*."

A week later, Aka said the first time he put out a batch of Moke's pickled turnips in a Hawaiian smorgy, between the *Huli-Huli* Chicken and the *Kalua* Pig, they were consumed before the buffet period was half over. He placed a large order asking for different types of pickled vegetables. Shortly thereafter, Kamaki got other hotels from Princeville to Poipu to begin ordering.

Lina and Kamaki sit on their rear lanai a lot now as trade winds rustle the palm trees. Kamaki cut a gate through the fence that separated their rear yard from Moke's. From the trees in his yard, Moke brings chilled coconuts with their ends lopped off, ready to drink. Finally, the neighbors became ashamed of how they treated Moke, especially the man who took Moke's pickled turnips home to his wife.

Moke had finally been able to afford a garbage disposal and some new clothes. He got his teeth cleaned and whitened, but still hides his smile behind a hand because he is not used to flashing pearly whites. He's looking to buy a small pickup, after which he would donate his tricycle to the senior center.

Kamaki fertilized the soil in Moke's back yard and got it healthy again. He and Moke grow vegetables and also maintain the landscaping in both yards. Orders for Moke's pickled vegetables have grown large, so Kamaki takes him shopping at the farmer's market. Lina put together a cookbook of Moke's strange and *ono* concoctions hoping to get it published. They decided to call it *Pupule Island Recipes*.

To Soar

I wish I were a bird, a powerful eagle, maybe a white dove, or I'd settle for being a goose because a gaggle of geese are a cohesive lot that support one another as they fly in V formation with each taking a turn in the lead to cut a trough through the air as the others ride in the wake which enables them to rest and ultimately fly farther like we could have so that we could attain potentials unreached before in this little world of endless sorrow and woe that I am locked into and keeps me wishing to soar as you in your world seem to have it all and go about your days smiling in secrecy and leave me alone to hold together the fraying bits of our lives without so much as gratitude because we simply do not speak; you for fear that you might make a slip of the tongue about where you've been and me because I've remained a caged, frail prisoner of conscience far too long, but now I plan to soar because I followed your car with me the free bird driving mine until I saw where you lay low yet could not reason why; while I remained at a distance imagining you experiencing stolen moments of ecstasy that do not include me because you and I have lost the desire to feather the same nest except when you drop your dirty social laundry on me and expect me to protect your public image once more which makes me again wish to be an unencumbered bird and all too often I do escape to soar above the rooftops and trees and into the clouds to feel the wind and rain cleansing me of your indiscretions and restoring the life that is mine which is freer than yours in your clandestine little world because it is exactly that, little, as I being in denial flying in my car follow you night after night as if I have to feel the pain again and again to make me stop my escapism and to free myself from the confines you have built to keep me grounded so I can truly be that graceful bird soaring up and away from the state of confusion that you have brought upon us because out there where I am free I have found new strength through the grace of imagined autonomy that gives me courage to hover again and again near that house where I watch the shadows on the blinds and see the lights go out and later come back on dimly just before you leave to return home as if you owned the world in which I also live and where my imaginary flights have strengthened me as I plan to soar and no matter that I am awkward like a goose, what you will be left with after this free bird swoops down is the mess that I'm about to drop on you.

Out of Body

I ran as fast as I could. *I'm not part of this!* ricocheted inside my brain. Just another guy on the street. Although I had the advantage of being under the cover of night, the sound of hastened footsteps behind drew closer and no matter which way I turned, which way I ducked and darted, the footsteps dogged me. I slipped through one doorway that stood slightly ajar and out the back of the building, through the alley and across another street.

Damned streetlights, damned neons!

Another alley, another street, and another chance to escape a madman who saw me as a threat. I saw nothing and only heard the shot. The scruffy guy who tried to panhandle me fell and a throng of people rushed in and crowded me out. I didn't know from where the shot rang out or who the shooter had been. I was waiting for Karen, who was late from apartment hunting with her friend, Ruthie. Within seconds, a black sedan sped toward me where I stood. From behind darkened windows with one lowered halfway, the barrel of a handgun pointed straight at me.

I ducked. The bullet hit the wall behind me as the car kept going. Bewildered, I should have fallen to the ground. They would have kept going, but before they crossed the intersection, a passenger wearing a white tee shirt and brandishing the gun leaned his whole upper body out of the window and craned his neck to see if I was hit. I trembled in shock wondering why someone would take a potshot at me. The panhandler looked like a druggie and it might have appeared that we were together. The guy with the gun jumped out of the car and began to run back toward me as the driver cracked a U-turn in the middle of traffic that whizzed in both directions. I was glad Karen was late.

That was the last glimpse I saw of the shooter before I began to run. Why did Karen choose to meet on a street known for drive-by shootings? I hope she's not considering living in this neighborhood.

Another shot rang out and a woman I ran past jolted from a bullet that sprawled her backwards onto the pavement. Other people saw what happened and rushed to help. I kept running. That idiot meant business. I ducked into a doorway and knew I'd been had when all I saw were two doors to restrooms and no place to take cover. The clock behind the counter showed a few minutes past eleven p.m. I forced my way past two waitresses at the corner of the counter.

"Help!" I said. "Call the police!"

I had to find a place to hide. I ran into the kitchen and spotted two guys carrying garbage out through a rear doorway. I shoved my way past them and into the alley.

I squatted in the shadow of a dumpster next to an alcove stacked with wooden fruit crates stagnant with fermentation. I expected the shooter to bolt out of the kitchen but only the two employees stepped outside to dump their trash. I wondered where the shooter had disappeared. I had placed myself between a dumpster and the crates facing the open end of the alley at the street. As I looked toward the street, what I feared happened. The man in the tee shirt bolted into the window of light and stopped. He scanned the long narrow alley. Light reflected off his sweaty skin but I couldn't make out his features. Brazen he was, standing there with the gun pressed against his thigh.

TV had educated me. I can tell when someone in pursuit carries a gun, cop and criminal alike. The gun arm is locked rigid in an almost vertical position. The gun is pointed to the ground at their side, even points a little backward. The other arm crosses the chest and supports the arm with the hand holding the gun. The pursuer leans forward, ready to pounce. The arms and gun are the only parts that don't bend into the crouch. To covertly maneuver around, they hobble like a lame animal.

He crouched and jockeyed into the alley. Pointing the gun straight out ahead, he rotated from side to side as he panned the area. My pulse raced as if my heart was about to burn out. I folded my arms across my chest and buried my fists deep into my armpits and turned my face backwards toward the corner of the dumpster so my skin wouldn't reflect light. Why was that crazy pursuing me? I held my breath and hoped the man wouldn't hear me breathe. I froze to the spot and hoped he wouldn't hear me sweat. I was right there in the slotted shadows of the fruit crates, a little more than a hundred feet or so in front of him, with the dim lighting in his favor. My hard-soled shoes began to slip on the grunge of the alley floor and I almost lost my balance as I squatted.

Something moved behind the dumpster at the other end. More adrenaline pumped and the charge could only route through my nervous system like crazed rats in a maze.

Rats!

Two huge rats foraged behind the dumpster. If they fled the shooter would spot me.

From the back doorway of the restaurant I heard, "Hey, get out of here, punk! Get away from here!"

Sirens wailed, tires screeched. I dared a peek between the slats of a crate. Intermittent blue lights flashed their circular pattern. Excited people crowded the street. The police and, hopefully, medics had arrived to tend to the victims. The creep straightened, tucked the gun into his waistband and pulled the tee shirt loosely over it. One last look and he turned and strutted toward the alley entrance, acting nonchalant.

Since the cops had arrived, I'd be safe. The shooter wouldn't dare take out anyone in front of the police and the crowd.

As the shooter walked, I jumped from my hiding place sprinting back to the kitchen doorway. Then my nerves went raw. I saw the shooter catch a glimpse of me. His head jerked back in my direction. I heard the shot and time kicked into slow motion like electrical power being unexpectedly cut.

* * *

Something slams into me from behind but I barely feel it. My body jolts in a slow motion charade that seems will never end. Already in motion, I'm sent flying in a long wind glide. I land hard, head first, and feel a corner of concrete slice into my forehead. The vertebrae in my neck crackle. I crumple face down but don't physically feel any of this. The pain comes slowly because I'm already detached from what's happening. I'm beginning to shake as if I'm inside my body but not attached to the outer shell. The vibration makes a noise that sounds like the rough sides of two rocks being coarsely grated together as I begin to lift. An ominous buzzing fills my head and ears. I'm vibrating severely as I exit through the top of my head. I see a person lying crumpled in the alley as I hover above. I lift higher and higher and see two men running from the restaurant toward the body sprawled on the filthy concrete. Police at the alley entrance throw a man in a white tee shirt to the ground and wrench his arms behind him. I realize how high I've risen. My ascent seems effortless and normal.

The images on the ground disappear as if diluted into oblivion. Strangely, three large golden orbs above me burst with muted popping sounds as I ascend through them. The void fills with radiant white that changes to endless glowing hues I've never before seen. When I focus on the new colors, I'm filled with the realization that this is unimportant and I float still higher. That's the last time I am able to think of much. My emotions and rationale are fleeting. I simply... am.

A glowing that has no end envelops me and I know nothing but total peace. I am more whole now than I have ever been. I perceive in every direction at once, having no limitations of front, back or sides. The radiance persists as far as I can sense and probably beyond. I am simply inside the all-encompassing light with it inside of me. I am at one with it and feel total peace the like I've never known.

My head feels unusually gorged with a new kinetic energy. With that thought, I realize my ability to rationalize is returning. I'm feeling my emotions again and find it disappointing. I sink... sink... down out of the radiance. *Wait!* I want to cry out. Why was I shown this if I can't stay? I sink and sink until, as if peering through a softly lighted tube, I again see the body on the ground. The clothes have been cut away and lay nearby in a shredded heap. It's completely naked except for a large square patch of white over the lumbar area. As the police watch, two medics place a harness around the body's neck and place a board over the body and securely strap the body and head to it. They roll the body and board over in unison so the body is face up.

My dismay grows. I'm sinking down out of the glowing and can't stop myself. Slowly, I realize I'm re-entering the body on the ground. I slip easily back in through the top of its head and settle in near the solar plexus. My senses come alive again with tingling like every cell had been asleep. The brilliant glowing begins to pull back in toward the center of my being like a light withdrawing back into its source. The last remnants of radiance dissipate in the air around me as well as inside me in bursts like miniscule stars exploding into a million more.

* * *

"Pity," someone hovering above me says. "Close to the spine."

I can't stand the pumping pressure on my chest. I choke and retch. Air floods my lungs.

"Hey, we've got him back," she says as she presses fingertips against the side of my neck. She puts an oxygen mask over my mouth and nose and I breathe a whole lot better.

My body tingles and I barely endure the nervy feeling. I want to shake my legs and arms but find I cannot move. My head feels like it's rocking back and forth and is still full of the new current I picked up in the light. My thoughts run amuck and time seems stretched, but judging from the movements of the medics, it just seems slow because my mind is racing. My emotions run the spectrum from shock to elation, often stalling in the high. In spite of some prickly feelings, I remain detached from my surroundings and could get to like this heady sensation if it can keep away the confusion.

Fingers probe and needles prick. My senses seem heightened and raw. The smell of a damp alley was never so putrid, dingy brick walls never so vibrant, voices never as piercing, and night was never so translucent.

I'm lifted on the board and carried away. Sirens blare.

The prickly feelings persist, especially in my legs. I see inside myself as tiny stars continue to implode throughout my limbs and body. I'm vaguely aware of simultaneous universes within and without, the one within, glowing, ethereal, inviting. A guy dabs at the top of my forehead and comes up with bloody gauze.

"Can you feel this?" the female medic asks.

I try to see and, by her movements, know she jabs the soles of my feet or flicks at my toes but I don't feel it. The pain in my back seems distant, as if belonging to someone else. The current in my brain keeps me occupied as if pain is unimportant.

"You'd better log this," the man says as he applies constant pressure on my forehead. "What time did we reach this guy?"

"Eleven twenty-four."

"Karen," I say. I wonder if she ever showed up. The man lifts the mask but my thoughts are fleeting. Random shooting. Senseless. Karen's always late. "At least she didn't get shot."

I begin to understand what happened—that at the moment I was shot my soul left my body for an interlude in Spirit. I must have had a near-death experience. I'm awed and yet have to accept my body again, but in spite of endorphins protecting me, I refuse to accept that my legs may be paralyzed.

Clinging to the memory of my heavenly visit, what I want to do is escape the ills of life and return to the radiance I didn't know existed until I was out of my body. Why hadn't I seen the tunnel of light that people report seeing when they die and come back to tell about it? What pulled me back to physical consciousness? With the streetlights behind him, I hadn't seen the perpetrator's features. Certainly I wouldn't be able to later identify him. I'm young and in the prime of life, but I have no unfinished business as far as life goes. People die unexpectedly all the time and life goes on. Why was I made to return to a broken body or any body, when all I wish for is to stay in Spirit?

With the thought of Spirit, I revel in the hyperactive intensity of my mental processes. In addition to simultaneous myriad thoughts, there's still that ominous buzz inside my head and ears that, surprisingly, is calming instead of distracting. My mental acuity has been accelerated into high gear. I am an observer watching my thoughts race on with enough speed to power a row of turbine engines. The ambulance sways and rocks in its flight. The medics jostle around and hover over me. I am only a smiling observer sinking with awe into an ethereal abyss while watching them in that other realm.

Thoughts are questions. Why had I not been truly able to disconnect from the world? Like when I realized that, in Spirit, I was at peace for the first and only time and that earthly happiness fades to nothing in comparison. I must have had something with which to compare that thought that kept me attached to worldly consciousness. And colors—how did I know those were colors I hadn't seen before unless I remembered colors I already knew? Those were colors I can't describe with earthly words. Why hadn't I seen departed loved ones like people claim when they have a near-death experience? Had I really almost died?

For the moment, I choke up and want to scream profanities at life, the real purpose of which I now admit I know nothing at all. Again, I see the medic touch my legs but can't feel her fingers probe. The thought of paralysis filters in and I thrash and scream, "I don't want to live with a broken body!" The mask on my face muffles the words but the glut of kinetic energy in my lips keep them from moving properly anyway. They quiver and twitch and make me stutter as if I'm cold. Yet, every time I try to attack my anguish with hatred and ire, the negativity is dissolved before it has a chance to fester.

My thoughts race on, seeming to elongate time as understanding pours in. Something cathartic is taking place. In addition to vanquishing negative emotions, I think I can accept my predicament as my mental agony is dissolved by a power that leaves me mystified. If my mind playing tricks on me is a by-product of natural endorphins, I say, so what? Bring on those numbing hormones. I feel too good to feel bad.

My mind is glutted with indescribable hyperactivity. Instead of asking endless questions, I find myself calming. Each single thought receives clarification, each unfinished thought, an ending. The knowledge enters my mind that I wasn't meant to die but had an out-of-body experience instead. I wasn't meant to die.

Mentally, I grope for thoughts that might help me understand what's happening. Vivid remembrances of Ruthie, whom I met through Karen, and who turned me off because of her belief in higher consciousness, parade from memory.

"Ruthie," I nearly yell as I realize why she comes to mind. "Ruthie." My dislike of Ruthie's beliefs had forced a tentative wedge between Karen and me.

The attendant lifts the mask. "Is she your wife?" the guy at my head asks. "Sir?"

"Remember that name," the woman says. "He said 'Ruthie.' "

"Yeah, and I think he said 'Karen' earlier."

"…caused by trauma—illness—deep meditation…." Ruthie had said that.

"He's incoherent," he says, replacing the mask.

"Sir, can you tell us your name?" the other asks.

Ruthie had a horrifying experience and later said her mind had been running full tilt ever since.

"Psychotic," I say softly.

"What's that?" the attendant asks as he lifts the mask again.

Doctors called Ruthie's episode a psychotic break caused by the trauma of rape. Her only solace afterwards was to go deep into meditation where she had an out-of-body experience. "Not psychotic," I say, remembering that Ruthie had been found suffering no psychosis. Since the occurrence, she had written several papers about her experiences and someone evidently thought her credible enough to begin charting her greatly enhanced IQ. "The human mind," I say as my tears spill out. I strain. *Why can't I move? Let go of me!*

"He's delirious," the man says. "Rambling."

"Combative too," the woman says.

I had treated Ruthie poorly, hadn't believed her. When we met, she was reading books about the wonder of the human brain and how ordinary people can transcend physical limitations.

"It's clear," I say. This time the attendant doesn't lift the mask. I try to flail my head but feel the man's hands holding it firmly in place. The odor of drying blood crimping the skin on my face seeps under the mask and stinks.

"Don't try to move any part of your spine," he says.

Ha! I'm unable to move any part of me. I cry out, and yet feel foolish because through all this, each time I take my attention away from the current in my head, I only want more to return to it. I take a deep breath and resign myself to knowing that something else is going on, over which I have no control, and which relentlessly seesaws me back and forth across the realm of sanity.

As I remember my conversations with Ruthie, waves of confirmation wash over me. I had not had a near-death experience. It was an out-of-body-experience and I owe the understanding of it to that woman. I owe her an apology.

"Her name—what was her last name?"

Through normal processes of the human mind, I've just been given a peek into a higher realm of consciousness. My body may be broken but my mind has metamorphosed. My spirits soar. The human mind, through the brain, is capable of such an accomplishment.

I'm being lifted out of the ambulance. The attendants and several others wearing white run with me on the gurney down a corridor. That damnable antiseptic hospital smell gags me. Noise levels rise and send me fleeing inwards. I close my eyes to shut out the glare of the lights.

"Single gunshot wound to the lumbar," the woman medic barks to new attendants. "No exit. Laceration and hematoma above the right temple, possibly a small bleeder. Patient is delirious, combative. Pulse is thready, pupils—"

"Trauma Bay One," someone yells.

Mentally, I check out as I remember clips of emergency room TV shows with everyone talking at once, frantically barking orders, the pokes and sticks of needles. I've seen it all and now it bores me. I want to flick the channel. I struggle to move and speak. More hands hold my head in place. These people need to know I'm okay. Someone else holds the remote as I'm backed up and plugged into things. Or they into me. I concentrate on the woman who has been my saving grace. "Ruthie," I say.

"Sir?" one of the faces hovering above me asks. "Can you hear me? I'm Doctor Malcolm, a neurosurgeon. I'm gonna take a look at your spine."

A nurse lifts the mask. "What's your name?" she asks. Voices seem to come from another world and stab into my sensitized brain.

My mind begins to swim. "Ruthie," I say again. My mouth is dry, yet I feel clammy. "Karen...."

"Sir, what's your name?" she asks again.

I don't reply because I'm smiling and can't help thinking that it doesn't really matter. None of this matters. My arms are freed but moving them feels like learning how all over again. The energy that numbed my lips has also filled my limbs, glutting in my hands and fingers and rendering them sluggish.

"We're going to move you," a face hovering over mine says. "Don't try to help."

Me... help? I'm lifted and scooted and land on a more comfortable surface. I'm as limp and sluggish as a wet piece of paper and have about as much feeling. I need to let them know I'm okay but have as much input as I do watching one of those TV shows. It dawns on me that I am not my body and that prospect fills me, literally, with waves of joy. By the stunned looks of the attendants when I revel in momentary delight, they must think I'm nuts. Why do they keep asking me what's going on? They wouldn't understand if I knew how to explain.

"Can't sedate him till we learn what's causing his delirium," Dr. Malcolm says. He turns to an eager looking young guy draped with a stethoscope and who looks more like a child playing doctor. "What's your take?" he asks.

Don't let that kid cut on me!

"Could be spinal shock if the cord's been insulted," the kid says. "Could also be lack of blood flow to the brain."

I'm not delirious. I thought I had screamed it but my mouth hadn't moved and no one took notice. I try to grab someone for attention. My arm is pinned down again.

A policeman standing nearby holds something familiar and reads. "Name is John Marks. Age, thirty-two."

Hey, that's my wallet. As I make the connection to something of mine, the energy intensifies again and I begin to feel as good as when I had been out in the ozone. The energy stabilizes and goes into whatever you concentrate upon, Ruthie had said.

"Would you look at that?" someone says. She giggles and points to my groin area and the men chuckle.

Wondering what is so startling, I try to lift my head to see, but feel an uncomfortable pulling shoot up the length of my spine and stab into my brain. I cry out and fall back, but not before I see the meager cloth covering my pelvic area lift a little. The movement I made and the uncertainty of what was happening sent my head reeling. That new current coursed through me again and I saw it as if I had x-ray vision into the ethereal realm that surely exists inside of me.

"He's got an erection," someone says.

"Aha, the ol' sudden sympathetic-parasympathetic nervous system discharge," the kid doctor says.

The new energy stimulates the brain, makes you overly horny, Ruthie had said as she laughed. I thought she had exaggerated, a con to get me to see things her way.

I lift my head and wail, "The energy is real." But why can't I feel my own erection? Someone pulls my head down again.

"I wonder if he'll remember any of this," a nurse says.

Why hadn't I felt my own erection, since stimulation has always been a motivating factor in my life? My anger flares. I don't want to be paralyzed. Not now, now that the mysteries of life are within reach.

I want to lash out. Karen would have stayed with me tonight. She would have. I thrash. The multiple IV lines dance like loose clotheslines in a storm. "I want out—have to find that woman." I struggle to sit up, have so many questions. Hands restrain me.

More poking and probing as a thin needle-like piece of gleaming metal is stuck into the soles of my feet and walked up the length of both legs waiting for a response I can't produce. Poked above the hip, I yelp. My frustration flares as I realize what I direct my thoughts to intensifies in this new state.

"We need to find out why he's combative... delirious," Dr. Malcolm says. "If there's spinal cord damage or lack of blood flow to the brain, sedation will only mask it."

"Are you in pain?" a voice asks.

"Mr. Marks? Hey, John," another woman says. "Calm down. We're going to roll you over. Relax. Don't try to help."

As if watching TV again, the doctor huddles behind me and comes up with bloody, gloved fingers. That blood is mine, but why didn't I feel him stick his fingers inside my back? "Hey," I yell through the mask. No one listens.

"Okay, get him to X-ray, stat," the doctor says. "Then straight up to OR."

As I lay motionless for the CT Scans, the softly lit tube-like structure I'm pushed into reminds me of the cylindrical hollow through which I returned to the body after my odyssey. A great peace fills me. Time to get my bearings. When I try to take stock of where I am and what's going on, internal light rushes in and shows me different pieces of my life for which I have no answers, and answers come. When I divert my mind away from the stream of mental activity to think separate thoughts, the stream continues still. Simultaneously, I receive information on different levels and finally, I'm so awed at the wonder of the brain that I can't stop the tears. The mental capability I had hoped for in life is right here stabilizing inside my head. I'm getting an overdose of the enhanced mental capacity that Ruthie talked about.

Being prepped in the operating room, I no longer wear the oxygen mask. I'm seeing everyone in a different light. Literally. Auras, Ruthie had called them. "Auras," I say as loudly as I can. "Auras." Said she could tell a lot about people depending on their glow. I didn't believe her, but I'm seeing auras and everyone in the room glows differently and it has nothing to do with the room lighting. I want this heightened acuity. I want it forever, no matter how the nurses look at one another and shake their heads in pity. I smile at one nurse and she sympathetically pats my arm.

After another examination, Dr. Malcolm says, "In his condition, we won't need anesthesia." Two nurses roll me over. I catch a glimpse of the clock. 11:55 p.m. Mentally, I check out on a vibrant stream of thought because I have no idea what gruesome thing they'll do that would normally require deadening. I can't feel my body below the hips anyway and need to get away from that prospect as well.

My thoughts are diverted back to the present when I hear the doctor say, "We're seeing too many of these." I hear the clank of the bullet drop inside a metal pan. "Single-round nine-millimeter surplus military bullet. Luckily, they don't expand."

"Single round? A shooter without an Uzi?" someone asks. "How archaic!"

Their laughter assaults me in waves as if someone turned the volume of a stereo up and down again and again. Hilarity in an operating room? Truly these people have seen too much of this.

"Bit off a chunk of the L-4, then ricocheted into a muscle," the doctor says. "Pretty clean wound, not a lot of damage."

"This one's lucky," someone else says. "But look at the condition it's left him in."

After a needle is poked into my forehead a couple of times, the choking stench of cauterized flesh reaches my nostrils. I roll my eyes upward and, from a new direction, watch a seamstress sew, the skin on my forehead her fabric. It's curious knowing I'm being scorched and patched and rolled onto my back unable to feel any of it.

"Only time will tell," the doctor says. "Let's get him to Recovery."

"Not so fast," a nurse says. "Look... look!" So I try to look too. "His leg lifted," she said, "He started to bend his knee." She taps my leg though I only see and not feel her do it. "Again," she says. "C'mon, move it again."

Nothing happens and I collapse backward clinging to the memory of my spirit odyssey for comfort.

"He needs time to heal," someone says. "Reality hasn't set in yet."

I can't be paralyzed. I just can't be. Some force inside won't let me cling to negative thoughts. My mind carries a new breath of life. In spite of my trauma, I'm feeling better than my best self again.

Finally left alone in the dimly lit recovery room and listening to the vibrancy of silence, the new energy pulsates inside my brain. My mental processes still function at such an alarming rate that my senses remain raw. Every once in a while, I perceive a glimpse of what surely must be the gross reality of this situation that one nurse mentioned and I begin to shake uncontrollably. I'll have to control my fright if I'm to understand all that's happening. I'm not going to listen to anyone telling me I'm paralyzed.

According to what Ruthie had said, in spite of the energy slowing down a bit after a few years, the process lasts and because of that, she had found a new level of intelligence. Is that what I have to look forward to? Anything you put your mind to will be intensified, she had said. Oh, please, let it be so. I'm concentrating on walking again.

The woman whose very sanity I scoffed had been right. I've got to find her. I've been awakened to the real reason to live and it's right inside my brain.

The clock on the wall says 12:58 a.m. In a little less than two hours I've had a peek at both heaven and hell and continue to witness energies inside my body that doctors never see. Though I've gained something yet indescribable, I presently cannot feel my lower half and push away the thought that it'll be a while before I'm normal again.

A door opens and I struggle to turn my sore, stiffening neck muscles to look in that direction. A nurse shows someone in. It's Karen. She hesitates, looks at me strangely. We might have been lovers tonight. I remember wearing a trendy new suit I bought to impress her. The idea comes to me that the shooter might have thought I was a rival gang member working his territory because my suit was dark. Karen finally comes close to the bed but doesn't reach to take my hand.

"I arrived just as the ambulance took you away," she says as she holds her arms locked at the wrists against her stomach. Her aura is pulled in real tight around her. She doesn't light up the room like some of the doctors and nurses. She isn't crying or emotional. She's too aloof and just going through the motions. I don't have a chance with her now. Bubbly, active, on-the-move Karen won't want half a man. She's already shut me out.

Another moment of reality sets in. Who'll want me in this condition?

Wishful thinking causes a lump in my throat and I feel pathetic as she stares. I thought that at least she'd take my hand. Another reality check. Things are changing too fast. Well, I'm not letting her or this set-back keep me down. I've got a new life to live. I'll find Ruthie.

Bit off a chunk of the L-4, the doctor said. Ricocheted into a muscle. Not once did he say my nerves were damaged. I felt the nerves in my legs tingle just after I re-entered my body and later in the ambulance too. Though I can't feel my legs now, it may only be due to shock. I'm not going to be paralyzed. I'm going to keep moving and pick up right where I left off. If I'm to be confined to a wheelchair while I heal, I'll need one with a motor because I don't plan to vegetate. Reality can stay away till I find sanity again.

Once more, the door begins to open, but slowly. Brilliant white light pours in ahead of the figure of another person slipping into the room. What an aura!

Karen glances toward the doorway and then back to me as if nothing too unusual is happening. I'll bet she doesn't see auras. "While I was waiting for you to come out of surgery, I called Ruthie," she said, "to talk, because I felt so bad for you."

I focus on the other person. It is Ruthie. She smiles and comes forward. Karen seems relieved to fade into the background with her diminished aura while Ruthie's glow envelops and comforts me.

"You're healing already, aren't you, John?" Ruthie asks as she takes my hand.

The moment she touches me, a charge of bonding energy connects us. Ruthie had once explained that doctors had begun prescribing Healing Touch for hospital patients and that she had become a practitioner. *Oh yes, touch me again. Teach me.*

I choke back tears. I try to speak and can't. I want to thank her for coming. Yet, all I can do is weakly squeeze her hand and wonder what is happening to me. As quickly as I wonder, my mind tells me that what I have in common with Ruthie is very real. Like her, I'll study and write about my experience. The reality of what has happened tells me that if the mind is capable of accelerating, people should be able to reach this heightened degree of intensity and clarity without having to experience a trauma. I've had a new life thrust upon me, a new reality. The room glows. I'm here, I'm rational, and I'm sane, although like Ruthie, I may have a lot of trouble getting people to believe it.

Looking for a Life

In my teens, I liked hunky guys; in my twenties, hung with guys who were fun. In my thirties, I looked for a successful man; in my forties, for someone who held his looks and physique. In my fifties, I sought a wealthy retiree. In my sixties, too late, I wondered what I had to offer.

Most Wanted

"Take this precious child into your loving arms," the minister was saying. His eyes were closed as he clutched the Bible and tilted his face toward the sky.

Many people attended the funeral service and showed up at the gravesite for what could only be to pay the most final of respects. They came in a show of support. Some of their sons would be next.

Wind snapped the canvas awning but there would be no rain today. Just a week earlier, Jeremy had managed an innocent smile and was able to say the rain was over for the season. In spite of his lack of vitality and inability to move so much as a limb, he had said it with such an air of finality, as if the rain would never come again. His mother knew that the end was at hand for him. Still, she prayed for a miracle that would let her only child live.

With the weather finally warming, most people wore everyday clothes of varying colors. One didn't have to wear black to mourn anymore, but who was the gaunt looking man dressed in death's color from head to toe who hung back from the crowd? He paced between rows of headstones, stopping frequently to take long pulls on a cigarette. Some respect!

Jeremy was the third boy in the neighborhood to succumb to AIDS in a short period of time. No one knew how the boys had contracted the HIV virus. Some say it was the children's dentist, one of only two in their small town. The two who already died, plus Jeremy and the others that had crossed over to full-blown AIDS, had dental work done in the same office. Yet, that dentist had been tested and did not have the HIV virus; nor did his assistants, nor the hygienist. Even the sterilization procedures of his instruments had been scrutinized and no irregularities found.

"It came from somewhere else," Viviana said.

"Oh, Viv," Mavie said, whispering and leaning close and cradling Viv's shoulders. The metal chairs on which they sat clanked together as they shifted in the soft grass and earth.

"No irregularities?" Viv asked, barely choking out the words.

"About what?" Mavie asked. She leaned back into her chair but took Viv's hand onto her lap and held it tightly.

Someone firmly gripping her hand was like having a life rope tied around her while she was unable to hang on of her own accord. "My son," Viv said. "Killed by his dentist?"

"They haven't proven that," Mavie said, still whispering. "They're still investigating."

Viv could only hope for some answers. The wind blew fresh against her face and she was thankful for that. Not wishing to wear black, but deciding a spring dress would be inappropriate, she had worn a navy blue dress. The noontime sun beat down, and in spite of sitting under the awning, the heat was becoming unbearable. Viv felt as though she might faint. She wished to die to join her beloved son. Jeremy would never again breathe the fresh air that he loved as he skateboarded and played basketball or swam. Maybe the HIV was in the water in the public pool.

Frank sat mute beside her, more from shock than from having nothing to say. In his son, just experiencing manhood, lay his hope for the accomplishments he hadn't known. A pernicious HIV strain had quickly devoured their only child and his friends and turned them into zombies. This was what the other parents had yet to face.

"Too many boys with AIDS," Viv said.

"Let the living know that this child came into our lives," the minister said, "to bring joy and spread light as only a child can offer."

Why had investigators waited so long to interview the boys, waited till they needed a respirator and were too weak to care? What did those boys have in common that they weren't saying in order to protect one another? What guilt were they harboring? Had they made some sort of pact to protect those they were leaving behind from embarrassment or harassment? Surely, once diagnosed, each must have known the finality of their fate.

"First Scott, Larry a month later. Now Jeremy."

"Shhh," Mavie said.

"The doctors say Freddie's likely the next." Viv knew them all. After Freddie, Tommy might be next. Then Eddie. "All the boys played sports together."

Someone behind placed a hand on Viv's shoulder, a nice way of telling the mother of the deceased not to disrupt the service. She didn't care. She wanted to lash out but was too choked up to scream. Out of respect for Jeremy's last rites, she gritted her teeth and kept her mouth closed.

The man in black sauntered over near the foot of the burial plot opposite the minister. What was it about his eyes, a look of evil with his collar up against the wind? That image hiding behind the deep collar, mocking, almost strong enough to negate the minister's final words.

Momentarily, Viv thought she might be trying too hard to put the blame on someone else. "All I want is to know...," she said, whispering to Mavie more quietly as she also touched the reassuring hand on her shoulder.

"Shhh," Mavie said lovingly into her ear. "We'll talk after this is over."

"And so today," the minister said, "we lay to rest a child becoming a fine young man, full of curiosity about the wonders that life had to offer."

The man in black had disappeared. The hand on Viv's shoulder pulled back.

"Ashes to ashes," the minister said.

Her tears continued to spill over. Mavie guided her and Frank to where they were to stand. Everyone threw single roses onto the coffin or picked up and sprinkled lose earth. One by one, through her tears, the colors of the others' clothing came toward her. She heard their consoling words, yet their faces were a blur, and she could only nod. Even when she wiped her bleary eyes, tears continued, running freely.

The smell of stale cigarette smoke assaulted her nostrils. Who was he? She had to see his face close up. She dabbed at her eyes just before he grabbed her hand. He didn't shake it. The hand hung limp, like expecting her to take the initiative. His face was chiseled, a little too bone thin and sallow, like a walking skeleton. A chill went through her. Something about him made her think of the devil himself!

"I'm sorry for your loss, Ma'am," he said. Somehow the sentence didn't seem finished. It ended upbeat, as if he were gloating. Viv pulled her hand from his. He almost smiled as he stepped aside for the next consoler and quickly disappeared.

About a week after the funeral, Frank called to her from the living room. Other than watching the news and some nature shows, he and Viv seldom watched TV. It was Jeremy's toy. He preferred shows on Nova or the Nature and History Channels. The Hospice folks had removed every trace of their care of Jeremy and left no reminders. Those were in Jeremy's room, but the door remained closed. Yet lately, TV noises filled the void usually taken up with Jeremy's chattering about topics he found interesting and by his eagerness to get on with life.

"Viv!" Frank yelled again. "Come here! Hurry, Viviana!"

She went right away. *American's Most Wanted* was airing and Viv paid little attention, even as Frank implored her to sit.

"Why?" she asked. "We don't watch this stuff."

"Watch this time," he said.

So she did. She saw nothing she needed to know. America's Most Wanted had been responsible for the capture of yet another perpetrator. She was thankful for that. "Frank, please," she said, begging. "We don't need this kind of distraction."

"Watch!" he said.

The next segment to air was about a man named Logan Brooke who had assaulted boys in other states across the country. He had disappeared from the areas nearly ten years earlier and his whereabouts were unknown. An old picture of a man's roly-poly face flashed onto the screen. Viv's stomach felt squeamish at seeing the seemingly innocuous image of someone who could be a pedophile. The next flash of news made her tremble violently and almost faint in her chair. When the boys in California began dying of AIDS, each began telling their horrific stories. Logan Brooke had been positively identified as the man who spread the HIV virus to young boys on the west coast!

"Could that be it?" Frank asked, gasping and leaning forward in his chair. "Could it be him?"

Viv strained to see. If Logan Brooke had been infected with the HIV virus ten years earlier and had spread it, surely he would be just as close to his own demise. If that round pasty face, that now seemed vulgar, could be artfully drawn to have the look of death....

John Walsh spoke her very thoughts. "Even though the virus causes a person to wither, their bone structure remains the same. A forensic artist provided this rendition of what Brooke might look like today." The artist's rendering of a very sickly looking Logan Brooke flashed onto the screen.

Both Frank and Viviana jumped out of their seats.

"It's him!" Frank said. "He disappeared because he came clear across the country. He did it! I'll bet he did it!"

"That *is* him!" Viv said, screaming and pointing. "He was the gaunt man in black at Jeremy's funeral!"

Grandpappy's Cows

Grammy and Grandpappy had fifteen youngins o' their own, so I had me a mess o' cousins. Most of the boys looked the same, with straggly dirty blonde hair and mean squinty eyes. We girls was better. We looked different from one another by our hair color and sizes of our bosoms.

Grandpappy moved lots of us to a run-down trailer park near the railroad tracks. Him and Grammy lived in a doublewide next to the meadow 'cause they kept a milk cow. As neighbors moved out, more of our kin moved in. No matter the trailers was abandoned 'cause they was old, we was a family that stuck together. Pretty soon our kin took over every useable trailer in that danged weed-infested field. The poor folk thought we was rich.

Everyone who visited asked to go see the rest of them empty trailers. I sneaked and seen 'em already and they was empty, except for some mattresses the hobos left behind. When I asked why my uncles brought their girlfriends around to inspect those old trailers when they went out on dates, Grandpappy said, "They just want to bless our new home." Then he'd slap his knee and bellow till his eyes watered and he started to coughin'. He refused to let me go see with the other people and got downright nasty when I tried. "You stay put, li'l girlie," he said. "There's time enough to learn about life."

My daddy was a jack-of-all-trades and him and Grandpappy joined some of them trailers so's you could walk from one to another without goin' outside. When friends come over for some honky-tonkin', those old trailers would rock and once the rotted tires exploded on one of 'em.

Effie May was my closest cousin. She was older 'n me. The boys said she was built like a cow. Once when they headed off to the trailers, they said they was gonna go milk the cows. Like it was a dirty joke or somethin'. Effie May hung out with the boys a lot. She said they was her kissin' cousins.

One day, Effie May whispered to me, "They calm my yearnins, ya' know?"

I didn't know. I saw her and cousin Wilma Lou—who my momma told me to stay away from—go in and out of them abandoned trailers on the other side of the park with a bunch of boys time and again. Effie May was awful smart, said she knew how to be of service to folks. She always had money. But me? I didn't want to be nobody's servant. Me and my momma was close. I was blonde-headed like the rest of my kin, but my hair picked up some of my momma's red. I liked her the most, better 'n Effie May, 'cause Momma explained things to me.

As we kids was growin' up, I guess Grandpappy thought he still had to feed the whole brood. One day after Grammy gave away the old cow that dried up, he come home with another.

"I'm tired o' sittin' around all day shakin' the cream to the top o' that jar just to make butter," Grammy said.

"Well, we cain't afford the store-bought stuff yet either," Grandpappy said.

Johnny Jeb was one cousin continually up to no good. He used to squeeze the cow's udder so we could drink when we got thirsty while we was playin'. He'd squirt us just to be mean. We was lucky Grandpappy never knowed what the soggy stains was on our clothes and why leaves stuck in our hair 'cause after getting pushed in, we swam in the creek with our clothes on and he couldn't tell the difference.

"You grandkids is dirtier 'n my own ever was," he would say. "To think you live better off today."

Some of my aunts and uncles took a broom to their kids for coming home dirty. My momma just smiled and poured water into the old tin tub, throwed me a bar of Grammy's lye soap, and said, "You soak good now, Darlin'."

Grandpappy couldn't figure out why the cow didn't give much milk. He was attached to Bossie, his latest cow, and instead of getting rid of her, he brung home another.

Johnny Jeb loved that. He taught cousin Bobby Zeke to squirt and have milk fights in the meadow. When the rest of us got to laughin', we all learned to squirt.

Grandpa got a third cow just so's he could get enough milk together for our families every day. Anyway, between the three, they kept the weeds down real good. But it stunk some and the boys was put to scrapin' up the cow-pies and tossin' 'em into an empty field. Us girls stayed away from them dung fights.

Later on, when I started thinkin' about boys, I looked in the mirror to see what they was a-winkin' at. My bosoms finally growed like Effie May's. My kin said I wasn't bad looking and my hair shined like sunlight.

"Why'd you s'pose that is?" I asked my momma one day.

"Musta' been all that fresh cream you got in your hair when you was a kid," she said.

I never knew she knowed. I have a right smart image of my momma now that I know she let us kids enjoy the fun we had back when we was younger. I looked at her real hard 'cause I admired her more all of a sudden. Her brassy hair was so shiny.

My daddy said I matured real nice. He paced around lookin' at me like I was the chunk of gold that was gonna make him rich or somethin'. I wondered if him and Momma would let me go honky-tonkin'. Effie May said she could tell me how to take care of my yearnins.

The Boy at the Crossroad

My housemate Hal touched the back of his hand to his forehead. "Retirement's hard work," he said, feigning fatigue. "Let's go to the beach."

I slipped into my bathing suit and wrapped a short sarong over that and tied it off at the hip. We love to swim. Not only does it keep us tanned and healthy, it also keeps us thin and young looking in mid-life, despite the fact we both have graying hair.

We loaded up his van with snorkeling and beach gear and took off just as dawn came filtering in. Other than town and residential streetlights, the rural areas on the island of Kauai, as on most islands in Hawaii, are fairly dark at night.

As we approached an intersection of the highway bordering our small neighborhood, a boy about eight years old came into view. He moved about in an erratic pattern like he might be trying to catch something on the ground. He was alone.

"What the...?" Hal asked as he leaned forward and strained to see through the windshield.

The boy saw us approaching and headed for the curb. He turned around and started back to the other side. As we came closer, he stopped right in the middle of the road where it intersected the highway. Finally, he turned his back to us and stood with his arms tucked stiffly at his sides. He had very short hair and his clothes were neat and clean. I thought he might be out early in preparation for going to church.

Hal stopped along side of the boy and stuck his head out of the window and asked, "Are you okay?"

"I-I'm okay," he said. His voice was choppy. He took another step to leave and stopped; took a step in the opposite direction and stopped. He glanced at us sideways and rolled his eyes a lot. He wouldn't look directly at us, but opened his mouth a couple of times like he wanted to speak. He looked like he might cry. His lip quivered. I thought sure he was about to confess something. My motherly instincts kicked in. I wanted to sooth him somehow.

"What are you doing in the middle of the road at night?" Hal asked.

The boy's eyes flitted back and forth as he walked away and slipped around the rear of our van.

I called to him from my side window. "You sure you're okay?"

He took two steps toward us. "Uh… yeah," he said. "Sure." He held his right hand tight at his side, hiding something.

"What's in your hand?" I asked.

He wouldn't stand still. I thought he might flee. Finally, he hesitated a moment, then slowly showed me his hand. "Just my scissors," he said. His voice was flippant with guilt. He flopped the small scissors over a time or two to show me. The long sharp points gleamed. He closed the blades, and hastily threw the scissors into the pocket on his pants leg. Other metal tools stuck out and clinked together. In the early dawn, I couldn't make out what they were.

"Where do you live?"

His eyes got real big. He looked back down our street, seemed to choke up, but said nothing. He twirled a finger in his hair and pulled hard. I thought sure he would pull out a whole hank of hair. His lips quivered as he turned and walked back to the curb. Finally, he looked straight into my eyes. His eyes begged, but for what? What could he be doing in the middle of the road before dawn that would cause him such distress? I started to get out of the car to see if I could help him.

"I'm going home," he said as he took off running.

I stood beside the car and watched him duck into a back yard a little ways past our house. At least he was home.

On our way again, I asked Hal, "What could he be cutting outdoors at this hour? Creepy crawlers are the only things that move around at night."

"Don't jump to conclusions," Hal said. "He didn't have blood on his hands."

After a great day of snorkeling on the North Shore, Hal and I had dinner at our favorite local restaurant in Old Kapaa Town. Darkness was setting in as we approached our house, but it was still light enough that I saw that same boy on the lawn two doors down. I hadn't thought of him all day. Fiercely, he jabbed at a scrawny gray tabby that seemed cornered up a short tree. It didn't look to me as if he were playing. He must have hit the cat because it cried out angrily, loud enough that we could hear, and leaped out of the tree, bounding away limping. Something in the boy's hand gleamed. He started to take off after the cat but noticed our van and turned away and stood rigid before bolting into the back yard. That house was the only rental in our small neighborhood of mostly quiet families and retired homeowners. It attracted one transient family after another. Maybe his parents worked and left him alone most of the day.

After watching him viciously thrust at the cat and evidently injuring it, I couldn't help myself. I walked over and knocked on the door. The woman who answered could have been his grandmother. Her layered makeup and exaggerated false lashes seemed out of place in our humid, tropical climate. She wore a very large, loose, ruffled Hawaiian muumuu. She panted and puffed like it might have been an effort just to carry her hulk to the front door to open it.

"Your boy," I said, after introducing myself. "...was in the middle of the intersection before dawn and—"

"He's our neighborhood watch," she said.

I didn't know our area needed a security program. I must have looked confused.

She shrugged and the corners of her mouth twitched nervously when she tried to smile. Her thick beet-red lipstick filled the wrinkles at the corners of her mouth. "He keeps the area clean. Gets rid of the geckos for me. I hate those stupid lizards!"

"That's why he tried to hide his scissors?"

"Hide?" she asked. "He doesn't have to hide. What he does for me is kills those dirty geckos... those slimy toads too. I don't know where they come from but they're better off dead."

I remembered a conversation I had with my neighbor's husband just after I moved to Kauai. He told me about how geckos controlled the bugs and other pests that infest our homes, especially termites. The toads wouldn't hurt anyone either and they controlled the insects in our gardens.

The boy entered the room carrying a soda can and making gurgling, choking noises as he plunged his scissors downward in the air again and again as if stabbing something. He saw me. His eyes got real big and he did an about-face.

The woman turned and yelled, "I told you not to bring food and drink into this room!" Her living room was so immaculate it looked unused. She called him back into the room and he crept in, minus the can and scissors, and avoided looking at me. She wrapped her arms around him and pulled him in front of her. He stared at the floor.

"I just thought it was dangerous that he was in the middle of the intersection in the dark," I said.

"He wanders a lot," she said. "But he's a big boy. Kills those pests wherever he can find them, just lops their heads right off!" She made it sound like he was a real pro.

I began feeling queasy about the whole situation. "I guess I just wanted to make sure he was okay."

She smirked suddenly and pushed the boy aside. Sweat beaded on her forehead and ran down her temples. "So now… mind your own business!" Her abrupt attitude change took me by surprise.

"Sorry," I said, almost stuttering. "I was concerned for him. That's all."

She closed the door before I had time to turn and leave. I heard her scream at the boy, "Get the hell out of my living room!"

I couldn't get the boy or the strange woman out of my mind. Controlling pests in their own yard might be one thing, but not by beheading. Scouring the neighborhood in the dark with a scissors was a frightful scenario. I remembered earlier in the morning how the boy looked back down our street when I asked him where he lived. It seemed that he wanted to say something. He knew he was doing wrong but had no choice but to follow the dictates of that domineering woman and would pay dearly if he told.

Later, just as I was about to climb into the shower, I heard a commotion out on the street. A woman screamed, others shouted angrily, with children's high-pitched voices mixed in. I heard the grandmother's voice over the ruckus. I felt sorry for anyone who had to deal with her. I climbed into the shower. The neighbors could mend whatever they had gotten into.

Over the sounds of the shower water, I heard sirens approaching and once they were near, recognized them as from police cars. By the time I climbed out of the shower, I heard another siren, that of the firefighter paramedics. An ambulance arrived.

Someone knocked on my door. I dried quickly and threw on some clothes. My neighbor stood on my porch looking bewildered as she clung to her little girl's hand. "Did you hear the sirens?" she asked.

I looked down the street and could see the police car lights rotating but couldn't make out what was happening. It was dark already as attendants brought a stretcher out of the back of the ambulance. Police held back the neighbors. "What's that about?

"The new boy that just moved in," she said, gesturing toward the commotion. "He got into a fight with Andy, one of my daughter's friends. He raked a scissors across Andy's throat."

I gasped and realized my mouth hung agape.

"While I'm here," she said. "I also wanted to ask. Our new Persian kitten is missing. Have you seen it?"

Cafeteria Science

Between classes, if we students needed to pass time before the next session, the best place to relax and mingle was in the college cafeteria. That was where people watching could be developed into a talent. Friends jovially referred to the socializing as studying cafeteria science.

I frequently arrived early and sat by myself at one of the long tables and waited for friends to finish their classes. Several people I knew also took classes at the same times during the day. Other times, I would befriend someone from one of my classes, start a conversation and end up sitting with them. In addition to making great friendships, cafeteria science gave me some unique inspiration for papers for my psychology and creative writing classes, but one guy in particular I avoided at all cost.

Harvey, in his bigness and unwashed bib denim coveralls that wrapped around his sagging bulbous stomach, sat alone in his little vacuum at the far end of the cafeteria gouging fiercely at his fingernails. Every time he came up with a chunk of crud, into his mouth it went without checking to see what it might be; it was simply big enough for a bite.

Next he dug into his ears to shake something loose. Then his fingers disappeared up his nose. At regular intervals, the fingers went into his mouth. Did not pass go, did collect something, and went straight to the jail of his mouth. This guy would never get so far as to take a ride on the Reading or make it to Park Place or Boardwalk.

Next he thrust the flat of his palm deep into his armpits and couldn't do both fast enough. Each hand was brought up to his face in open fashion as he sniffed the palms and fingers.

My stomach convulsed. I wondered if anyone heard it groan.

Harvey and I work at the same company. We live in the same vicinity near work. Nonchalantly, I prayed it wouldn't happen as I secretly watched his eyes search around the room. I slouched down in my chair and my heart sunk further when he saw where I sat and promptly invited himself over to join me. My stomach flopped again. This walking creature made of animal, vegetable and mineral residue could make a mess out of my social image! The determined look in his eyes had a purpose. His gaze told me his thoughts: *There you are, friend. I'm going to sit with you before someone else does.*

The guy and girl at the end of the long table saw him coming and promptly picked up their books and papers and moved across the room. Harvey's odor preceded him. He plopped himself down beside me as I played like I hadn't noticed him. Heaven forbid if people thought Harvey and I were actually friends! Right away, I saw he had also missed the snack dangling out of his nose.

Turned toward me, with an elbow on the table and leaning too close, this guy with a sour breath took under a minute to point out that we could do ourselves a great favor by pooling it to and from college. I refused by telling the truth, that I had many errands to do before heading home after classes each day.

Nausea began rising from my stomach. I swallowed hard. To think he had no idea what he was offering to share—his vacuum—sucking up its chunks of crud! He assumed that we could be that chummy? My friends and I avoided him. We were afraid his stench might be contagious. It also hung in the air at work when he passed my desk. I had never approached him and avoided him as others did. Evidently ol' Harv couldn't see the world outside of his vacuity.

I visualized us in the car together, stuck in traffic, me driving, with Harvey the passenger laboring over his fingernails and having his breakfast. In the privacy of the car, I wondered if he might bring up his toenails.

At times, I wish I didn't have such an active imagination. I had just had my breakfast and thought I was about to lose it. I excused myself saying I needed to get to class early for a consultation with the instructor. As I hurried away, I wondered when big crusty Harv might finally determine he was ripe enough to have his annual bath.

Indoctrination

Straining to see as the craft hovers closer, I count five of them, which are two more than I expected. They look like otherworldly mannequins huddled together under a bubble. I can't be the only person who sees them. The office gossipers say I'm touched. They disbelieve the things that happen to me so I quit talking about them. Except for Frannie. She took a chance and hired the new girl in town. Said she saw something in me—whatever that was. She gave this racy girl a chance and I vowed I wouldn't let her down. I've become the top sales person in the shop. That's another reason the other ladies gossip.

The guy in the lane next to me toots twice and I'm distracted.

"Sure you can hold that thing on the road?" the honker yells from his car.

"I can do this in my sleep," I say as I throw him a sideways glance that lets him know he's sexist.

People say I'm bound to get into trouble one day. Unique is what I am and that won't be changing any time soon. I'm just me, leaving the honker behind in my dust, although my impulsiveness gets me into a jam once in a while.

I'm on my way to work on my motorcycle and trying to keep the bike upright as the flow of traffic starts and stops. Dragging my boot on the pavement helps keep my balance. I'm wearing leathers today but, at times, will wear a dress while riding. Nonconformist. That's me. People say I'm strange, or daring, or both. Who cares? I've got a job I don't intend to lose, and a rented townhouse a little too far away, but my commutes are exciting. I got started late today and threw on the first clothes I came to in the closet. Dawdling the minutes away trying to emulate a fashion hound cuts into my commute time. But now, waiting bores me because traffic has stopped again.

My mind wanders. Suddenly that silver disk with the bubble top quietly passes overhead in a silent tip and swoop motion. It's shiny and gleaming and about as wide as a couple of traffic lanes. Its outer rim diminishes to very flat around the periphery, just like described in those UFO sightings.

It's coming back. I raise my arm in the air, like I'd like to make contact. That would make my day. The glowing disk hovers above me and I reach for the edge and miss. The saucer re-positions. I finally get a grip and begin to feel so heady that my mind reels.

As we move in traffic, it stays with me, as if pulling me along. It's letting me hang on as I drive, sort of a friendship gesture, playing with me, I guess. How I shifted gears is unknown, considering it takes two hands to do so on a motorcycle. I wonder if other motorists can see this disk above me. If not, the other drivers must think I'm stupid for riding along with my arm in the air. I have to laugh.

I'm excited beyond belief. I knew we didn't have to fear these things. When I grasped the saucer's edge, I felt connected with it. It takes no effort to hold on as we move along together with me feeling more a part of their world than my own.

Traffic slams to a standstill and I wasn't paying attention. I let go of the saucer, but too late, unable to downshift fast enough. I swerve. My front tire nicks the car ahead and I see my bike crumple and I'm sent nearly riding the thermals. During the descent, my motorcycle appears beneath me and I flop onto the seat. Unbelievably, me and my bike are okay. So is the car I hit because no one's honking or stopping or panicking. Traffic crawls along, like it does every morning. Through the strange episode, I wasn't frightened, like I knew I'd be okay. So, did that really happen?

Having to let go of the saucer was disappointing. I felt connected to that ship and wished to get closer, even know the beings inside. As if they had heard my thoughts, the craft swoops and dips and hovers over me again before disappearing. When traffic comes to another stop, the beings materialize to my right, sitting in bumper-to-bumper traffic in a small car. Five unearthly, grotesque faces that raise the hair on the back of my neck morph into earthlings. These are not beings you'd want to meet in the dead of night. For a second, I catch a glimpse of tube-like structures protruding from their heads, writhing like Medusa's snakes. Their faces have long slits for eyes with something shiny and dark inside the slits. The rest of their faces are caved in, no noses, mouths or ears, only deep vertical wrinkles as if their heads were pulled away from the rest of their bodies. Something stuck out from top of their heads but I didn't have time to make out what it was. For sure, they must communicate telepathically. The images disappear and leave me wondering about my own mind.

My stomach quivers and sends a message that I should forget about this and leave well enough alone. My adrenalin surge fades after another moment of vertigo and I see them only as humans. Five guys. I have vague memories of seeing only three the first time. I know who they are, and they know that I know, as if they want the connection too. Every one of them looks about ready to break into laughter. They've always had a sense of humor, though I don't know how I know that. My focus changes when I notice their car. It's a brand new charcoal-black model of some sort of small coupe unlike anything made on this planet. If those aliens were going to materialize an earthly vehicle to give the impression they're human and car-pooling, they might, at least, have conjured one all of them could fit into. Was that a message about the idiocy of commuting? That's their kind of humor, poking fun at our reality. Flying saucers surely have no traffic jams.

The endless line of cars begins to move again. My sideways smile to them says *Thank you!* And, *I know who you are!* And, *What a thrill! Let's do it again!* Each smiles back. We have this little secret between us that doesn't fade from my mind. I hope they follow because I'm feeling frisky. It feels good to share minds with them, even to flirt with the whole carload, and it's all done with thought.

Arriving at the shop in a mall where I work, they have followed. As I'm walking into the building, the woman from the car behind me in traffic when I went soaring approaches on foot on my right.

I jokingly ask over my shoulder, "You didn't see any of that, did you?"

"Nah," she says. "I'm from Roswell, New Mexico. We're told we've never see a thing flying around and not to believe the myth about Hangar 14 either." She disappears through a doorway.

A voice seeming projected into my head says, "She's both envious and in awe... can only tolerate glimpses." I look around and see no one.

I'm singing the bouncy song that goes, *"I know... I know... I know...."* The aliens can hear me and it's like a silent message between us. It tells them I'm jubilant and at ease with what's happening. They're reading my mind, building trust.

Inside my work place, my co-workers are aware that I'm being watched.

"Look who's being followed again," someone says, her voice ringing with envy.

The aliens have parked at the curb, staying human-like, staying close, as if wishing to know my every thought. We're curious about each other and they're happy, too, that they've finally made a connection with an earthling who isn't afraid. How I know this escapes me, and I also remember glimpses of similar occurrences in the recent past. It's as if I'm being indoctrinated into a mind-blowing experience in small measures that are beginning to fit together. I want more!

I turn to look toward the curb and the whirling action fills my head with a reeling sensation. When the vertigo stops, my clothes are already changed and I'm presentable for the sales floor. My mind must have wandered from boredom in traffic. This has happened before and I couldn't figure out how I got from home to work without remembering the trip. Commuting on my bike sets me free. It's addicting! When I think about it, it's not just the bike ride that gives me this feeling. It's... it's something else.

"Okay, Dizzy," Frannie says. "Let's get started." She's the only one I allow to call me that. Work beckons, reminding that I must stop slipping off into these daydreams.

Later, pulling into my driveway at home, it's evening. I'm convinced that the episode with the space ship has occupied more than a few of my idle moments.

In the dim light of the garage, the thumb and fingertips of my right hand are coated with something shiny and silvery. It doesn't rub off. In fact it glows. This feels too, too familiar. Whatever I got on me today had better come off before I start cooking dinner.

Entering the hallway and intending to head straight for the washbasin, what greets me is a glowing fingerprint on the light switch that I hadn't touched. Another two glow on a nearby table. In fact, the entire living room is radiant with glowing blue-white marks. As I enter the room, multiple sets of silvery, odd-shaped footprints like suction cup marks appear on the floor at the front of my couch. They're here!

Another shot of adrenaline routs through my nervous system, the kind of surge that warns that something may have gone inexplicably wrong. I feel trapped in a body that won't move, but it's too late to figure a way out.

The footprints shuffle and turn facing me. Two sets begin to move toward me as the room fills with a burst of hauntingly cool, incredibly brilliant light that fades just as quickly. It's dark again, like indigo ink. I reach for the nearby table to steady myself and finding nothing exists to grab hold of.

All at once, another surge fills me, this time with both delight and dread. While I eagerly accept the adventure, an unexpected glimpse of those glowing, grotesque faces staring wide-eyed and casting laser-like beams through the dark and into me makes the pit of my stomach sink. The two step close, one on each side of me. Before I know it, their writhing tube-like structures have attached to my head! I'm nauseas, dizzy, about to faint, but no, this is different. I'm floating… floating…!

An Explosive Day

On the way to get my car air conditioner checked for a leak, I applied the brakes as I approached a stoplight. My car both grabbed and rejected the stop. I clunked along a few feet and then nearly slid into the car beside me.

The guy at the repair shop said, "One caliper is broken, the other damaged."

"But my car isn't even three years old," I said.

He gave me a ride to my favorite bookstore to wait out the repair. When I called a couple of hours later for a progress report, he said the car was overheating, causing the A/C fluid to spill out the overflow. My car has never overheated. I refused the expensive thermostat replacement till I could get a second opinion.

I took a sip of decaf from my mug and held it in the air in front of me as I tried to find my place in the book I was reading.

The mug exploded.

In less than a second, I was drenched in brown and the two guys at the table next to me were speckled. In the moment of shock, the only thing I could do was sit and stare at my hand that held only the handle of the mug.

In another instant, I was surrounded with hands wielding dishtowels and mops and I was being patted down and asked if I got burned.

The manager of these attentive people knew my favorite coffee and appeared with a complimentary paper cup and profuse apologies.

Once everyone in the café settled down, I lifted the paper cup to take a sip of fresh coffee and the plastic lid popped off in my face. Steam coated my glasses, but I caught what was happening before the cup tipped far enough to spill.

Later, in the bookstore, the manager and I were joking about the brown stains on my pale yellow sweater. "Was it a glass cup or ceramic?" she asked.

As I explained how it happened, the armload of DVDs she carried literally exploded from her arms and clattered over the floor. "I don't think I want to be near you today," she said as we both laughed.

After claiming my car and heading homeward, on a challenging stretch of road known locally as Blood Alley, a pickup flew past me and suddenly blew a tire. My brakes held.

At home again, I passed my bedroom as I headed for my office. I wanted to lose myself in the safety of work, but for some reason, I visualized my computer, my lifeline, crashing in a puff of smoke. I looked at my bed and wondered if I should just climb in and pull the covers over my head and wait for a better day.

The Smell of Death

Long ago, I learned a valuable lesson, though to this day people have thought it laughable. I've always known about death and when it's coming.

During my teens, my grandfather died. He was ill for a long time. I thought his odor was normal. Not until Auntie got sick did I realize the odor of Grandpa was on her. She died too. I told my parents about the offensive essence but they scoffed.

Throughout the years, when I was around a sick person, I knew if he or she would get well or die by the way that their odor progressed or disappeared. That scent permeated their clothing and tainted the air in their homes; a strong pungent effluvium of body chemistry drastically altered, as if from decay, but evidently undetected by people always with that person.

It's been over fifty years since I first smelled that odor and I've always been right. My husband and I have been together almost as long, although he recently chose seclusion, sleeping separately. Sadly, as I prepare to do his laundry, I detect that familiar scent on his clothes and in his room.

Legacy

When I fainted at my mother's memorial service, she would have teasingly said "Margaret, that's not like your mother!"

I had wished to be like her. As I matured, I found I needed my own personality and life. However, I still wished to emulate her ideals, attitude, and creativity. After years of hard work to support me as I was growing up, when she retired, Mother was finally able to manifest her personal dreams. The most important one was to paint.

I still have the many paintings she's gifted to me. I must say her latest ones are much more refined than her early ones. Still, I cherish them as a legacy of her enduring creativity. Mom had just begun to be known in the art world. After a few mini-strokes over the last 30 years, the big one took her. She passed away quietly in her sleep while on a trip to Seattle.

Back when I retired, I was already practicing my hand at painting. It seemed only logical that I do what came natural. Mom had a terrific influence over my interests, and my teachers said I had my mother's gift. Mom was ecstatic. "You're just like that painter Margaret," Mom would say, she having dabbled over the years. That was her name too. She named me after her, believing that we were part of the same soul and not necessarily separate souls as mother and daughter. How could she know that as far back as when I was born and needed a name? I think a mother's knowledge comes from another source to which only she is privy. As I grew older, I began to feel that I was being allowed to share in my mother's wisdom.

Dad was intimidated by Mom's perceptions. He had secrets, but not for long. It was as if Mom could read minds and it drove him nuts. They divorced when I was young and Mom went back to work. Dad died from a heart attack. After some years of working, Mom retired early and completely changed her life, which included her move to Hawaii.

As usual, she was right about us being like twins. She didn't have to encourage me. I simply was like her in nearly every aspect. Right down to the fact that my husband and I divorced because I was so energetic about life and he, known as a stick-in-the-mud, chose to go his bumbling way. I can only hope he made a good life for himself.

Seeing my mother's body laying dressed for a showing before her cremation drove the point home that she was gone. I stood close and gingerly touched her cheek, trying to sense her in that cold body. Her soul wasn't there, just her empty shell, no longer full of the warmth I felt when we hugged and pressed our faces together. The revelation that Mom was gone forever and that I was alone caused me to collapse.

I regret not visiting her, but she always traveled to my location. Every time she had a new piece of artwork that she wanted only me to have, she'd show up at my home in Phoenix, Arizona. If she showed in an expo in one state or another, she would take a side trip to visit me. We went on vacations together, each time meeting at a new location. We both carried cameras and enjoyed taking photos of subjects to paint.

Over the years, I had sent Mom several of my canvasses I thought she might like. My art was not as perfect as she might have produced, but she said the canvasses fit right in with her own art and she was proud to have them on her walls. She complimented me and passed along hints and clues about how to improve my capabilities. We'd sometimes talk for hours on the phone. We had just signed up for Skype, not only to save money but so she could demonstrate a technique or two.

Working and living far apart precluded frequent travel by me. Mom pinched and saved her divorce settlement and, along with selling her art, lived a stable life. My husband had nothing, but I wasn't dependent on him. I have made my own way and done it well enough. But, due to my long work days, I regret not visiting my mother at her townhouse in *Moili'ili* on the island of Oahu in Hawaii. Before I retired, I had been researching jobs that would enable me to move near her. After retirement, I had just convinced myself to move over with no thoughts of tomorrow, to just be spontaneous like she was. I love warmer weather. *The temperate climate in The Islands will suit us just fine,* Mom had said only days before she had her last stroke.

Mom left her worldly goods to me, but that cannot compare with all she taught me, perhaps more than I presently recognize. I stand in front of her townhouse, holding the urn with her ashes close with one arm, and her keys in my other trembling hand. I had wanted to visit her and be a part of this life with her. Why had I been so busy? Why hadn't I just taken the time?

From either side of the front steps, in small flowers beds, light and dark pink heliconia psittascorum on three foot stalks with long, lush green leaves wave at me in the breeze. I sense my mother's presence; can feel her in the artistry of the planting. The air is heavier here than the dry air in Arizona. It must be the humidity of which she spoke. A breeze wafts along and helps me feel freshened. The building façade is painted lavender with varying shades of darker lavender and purple trim. The beveled glass window in the front door, with its etched bird of paradise flowers beckons. As I take in the whole scene, what I'm seeing is an extremely creative artist's dollhouse. Tears flow freely. My throat gluts and my heart pounds. My legs wobble as I climb the few steps.

Walking slowly through the doorway, the delicate homey scent of the interior causes a rush of childhood memories and feelings. "Oh, Mom!" I say to the empty room. It's as if I've opened the door to a whole different world where traces of memories are preserved. On the floor inside the front door is her unclaimed mail. I scoop it up. One of the letters is from the *Kapiolani* Artists Creative. In bold lettering on the left side is printed *An Invitation!* I've received such letters. My mother would have been in this showing, I just know it.

Mom's living room is clean and neat, yet inviting, and decorated with yellow island-style bamboo furnishings, complete with soft green and blue floral print cushions and throws. Silk and wooden tropical trees and flowers brighten the alcoves. Her spectacular art pieces decorate the walls. The big red hanging Heliconia on a gallery-wrapped canvas, that she aptly named *Hot Flash*, is well placed on the side wall, the most conspicuous area in the room. Mom had said one art critic thought she painted similar to Georgia O'Keeffe, but I've studied O'Keeffe and Mom's talent was definitely her own. *Hot Flash* is huge, with three small but gorgeous complimenting floral canvasses, one above the other in totem on one side, but *Hot Flash* captures my attention. Just as I turn to leave the room, a thought jolts me. I look again at the smaller canvasses and gasp. "They're mine!" Those three smaller canvasses are the ones I gifted to her when I first began showing my work.

In the kitchen her pots and pans hang from a rack over the island stove. Mother really did remodel well. She had even painted Hawaiian cooking scenes in sepia fit for an island-style kitchen. On one wall under the cupboards she had painted two brown-skinned island men lifting a barbequed pig out of an *imu.* That's what she called it; an *imu*, an in-the-ground roasting oven. On the wall behind the table, three hula girls danced before a luau spread on the ground. The flowers they wore and the ones on the lower corners of the mural had red in them. Those were plumerias. Mom had sent pictures of those beautiful flowers. Mom knew what she was doing. This kitchen felt like a fun place to be. I can see myself cooking in this room. I can see Mom and me cooking together. I only wish....

Upstairs, her bedroom is also finished in lavender, her favorite pastel. Her *Balahe* perfume delicately lingers, the black designer bottle awarded center placement in front of the mirror on the dresser. Mom was only five feet, three inches tall; like me, or I like her. She didn't care for a king-sized bed. Her town house is small and the wide twin-sized Hawaiian *punee* bed with its hand-carved Koa frame surely served its purpose. A Hawaiian quilt of lavender plumeria designs covers the bed. Several soft lavender and purple flower paintings grace the walls on a backdrop of a woven *lauhala* mat. A tall silk banana tree with its reaching leaves simulate shade over the *punee.*

When I turn to leave, I spot her shortie nightgown hanging on the bathroom doorknob. Its delicate pink florals match the pinks in the bathroom. I can only stand and stare. I'm not ready to empty her closet.

Though I haven't yet been to the gabled crawl space in the attic, I know Mom wouldn't paint in any place other than a spacious well-lit area. The second and only other bedroom is at the front of the house, which faces north.

"Paint in north light, Margaret," she would say. "It's the only true light."

Again my hand shakes as I reach for the knob to the second bedroom. I take a deep breath and slowly open the door. What greets me takes my breath away!

Mom's huge easel sits to the side of the window. It looks as though when she painted, the sunlight would strike the canvas from over her shoulder. True light, she called it. So much art hung on the walls that every portion of space was claimed. Variations of every Hawaiian flower imaginable looks at me from the canvasses. I don't know how long I stood there, turning slowly to look at each and every piece.

To the left of the easel are more rows of finished canvasses, leaning back against others; to the right of the easel, the same. My mind is on overload. I spot her brushes, something she touched more than any other item in her possession. Mom was a bit compulsive. Her habit was to thoroughly clean all wet paint from her brushes at the end of the day before leaving them to dry. All her artists' tools were spotless, including the handles. Probably the last ones she used were the ones lying pointed downward from a small decorated ceramic wedge to keep fluid from settling into the ferrule and softening the glue that holds the bristles in place.

Mom's urn is still wrapped in my arm. I still hold her mail, feeling her close to me through these personal items. I stand shaking my head. This was my mother's life. All she ever taught me, I find in this room, this house. I'm unable to stop my tears. An incredible feeling overwhelms me. I feel at home here; my own home in Phoenix seeming nondescript and empty and may as well be in a foreign country. I want to live here. Thoughts race through my mind with lightning speed.

In the corner of the room sits a small white wicker desk with her laptop sitting to the side. Her white painting smock hangs over the back to the chair. The front is covered with splotches and dabs of many colors. I place her urn and mail on the desktop. Without thinking twice, and feeling compelled to put it on, I pull the smock off the chair and hurry to the bathroom. In the mirror, I see myself, the painter. Then I see my mother, and then I see myself again.

Back at her desk, two framed photos, one of Mom with two young children, hang on the wall behind. The other photo is of a group of young children. "Mom?" I ask as I bring the photo from the wall and study the proud smiling faces. In the picture, Mom shows that she had aged well. Her hair remained true blond. I run my fingers through my blond hair, as if touching might feel like touching hers again.

In the same photo, she is in the center with a pre-teen African-American boy on her left, a cherub-faced brunette girl in her early teens on her right. This is really puzzling, but only until I realize the message of the photo. Hanging on the wall behind the boy in the photo are several paintings of Africans, some in native dress. On the wall behind the girl are many small canvasses of birds and animals.

"Were you mentoring?" She hadn't mentioned teaching. I have a feeling there was much more to Mom and I'm soon to find out.

My attention is again drawn to mom's painting smock which I still wear. It fit me perfectly. My mother's essence is still present. This smock will always be hers, not mine. In time, I may frame it and hang it on the wall. It is so her. But for a while, it is also me.

I needed to open her mail, to pay bills and to clear up loose ends. The invitation to the art showing stated, "Your art leaped out at us. We hope your exquisite art will grace our showing by entering a few pieces in the Expo...."

That invitation told me Mom's life hasn't ended, even as I must organize a memorial service here in Hawaii.

File folders contained papers that indicated Mom was organizing a scholarship for underprivileged art students. I pause, shaking my head in wonder, unable to read through bleary eyes.

Unlike Mom, I have not had a child to whom to pass along this legacy. Knowledge and the ideals she stood for cannot end with me. I don't know how long I sat with my elbows on the desk and my forehead leaning against my knuckles. The sun had shifted and I had to turn on the desk lamp.

After much thought, I knew what I needed to do. The change would be a monstrous undertaking but one I want more than anything. Mom always said, "You can accomplish anything you wish, as long as you don't tell yourself you can't."

I'll be moving into this townhouse that Mom left me along with her few worldly possessions. I'll be showing Mom's art. I'd be honored if some of my pieces could be chosen to grace the showings next to hers in the future. Collectors who loved her work will buy the last ones left. The best pieces, however, I must reserve for my private collection and to use as examples to improve my own work and to teach. Mom has given me yet another gift.

Out of that thought sprung another truly wonderful idea. It happened quickly just as Mom would have decided. Why not? I'm part of her. The idea was that while I have no child to whom to pass along this knowledge, I can find one or more to mentor. I will establish this scholarship she began. I can also establish a trust in Mom's name to benefit more children in art. Mom's legacy will live on. Who else would carry it out but the daughter who is so much like her. "I can do anything I wish, as long as I don't tell myself I can't."

An Urgent Letter

Any Date
Ms. Hopeful Writer
Goddess of the House
Your Writing Niche
Nowheresville, Writers' World Unzipped

Dear Ms. Writer,

I was meant for writing. Each time you stick me into your mouth, I promise to stain your teeth.

Never mind thinking me faulty and changing the cartridge. I work well in all colors. You would look ridiculous with one black tooth, one red, one blue, and so on. That's unless you wish to incite a new fad of rainbow teeth. That would be as strange as the stories you create and might even garner you more rejection. So please, I'm not a pacifier and don't appreciate being salivated upon. You're stuck in suck mode and it's just another form of writer's block.

I suggest you learn to use your computer and keyboard, which you will be unable to get into your mouth, enabling you to get some writing finished. Save me for endorsing those royalty checks, if and when you can train your creativity to exit through your fingertips on the keyboard and not through massaging me with your lips and tongue. Start vocalizing that dialogue you're writing. Lay me on the desk before I drown.

Your Leaky Messenger,
Pen Teller

Rituals

Now that I'm single and dating again after nearly forty years of marriage, I'm finding I have a lot to catch up on.

"Jeffrey's not all there," my friends had warned.

As he and I became friends, I saw strange behaviors but nothing too unusual. For instance, at dinner, he would first eat his mashed potatoes, then the bread, and then the vegetables, followed by the meat. He avoided mixing foods, making sure ample space between different foods existed on the plate so they didn't touch. He ate all of one before tackling another.

"Why not combine tastes?" I asked.

"Guess I can't break old habits," he said.

After seeing him do this time and time again, it began to bother me a little. He would finish one entree, then pick up his plate and turn it so the next entree was directly in front of him. It seemed as if he ate the other foods first, in order to sneak up on the meat.

One evening after dinner when he put on his jacket, he stretched his neck like a goose, like the neckline might be too tight. Yet, the collar was open and in no way binding. These were strange behaviors, but everyone has rituals. I hoped my friends' warnings hadn't made me overly critical, but as time passed, I noticed other severe behaviors.

Every time we approached a crosswalk, he'd ceremoniously whack his fist four times against the black and white plaque with the arrow and that said *Push Button to Cross*. Only then would he push the button. After seeing him do this a few times, I must have looked doubtful.

"Hit the sign four times," he said. "The light will change in ten seconds."

"That's absurd," I said. "It's just a sign."

"A repairman told me that when I asked how to make the light change faster."

He believed the repairman who teased and played into his impatience? Not only was this strange behavior but so, too, was the belief in such nonsense.

People in cars at stoplights seemed puzzled when they watched him animatedly bang his fist. I got real embarrassed seeing him doing this. Passersby looked at us as if we were weirdoes.

As the weeks passed, I began to realize how deep his neuroses ran as I watched him for the umpteenth time stick a finger into his fly to make sure his zipper was up. Guys always do that. I do that, too, when I wear slacks, but not every few seconds.

That last time I saw Jeffrey, we happened upon a crosswalk button where the instruction plaque and screws were missing. Clearly nothing was housed behind the plaque to affect the light changing. It was just an instructional sign, obvious to anyone.

The button below the missing plaque was not damaged and still clearly usable. "Quick, hit something, Jeffrey," I said, teasing. "We have to get across the street."

He goose-necked again and stared at the empty rectangular frame attached to the solid metal light pole. Finally, dead serious, he fingered his zipper and turned and walked away. "It's broken," he said, calling out over his shoulder. "Let's find another place to cross."

Clearly, the missing sign saying to push the button to cross would not affect the use of the button. I pushed it and the light changed. At that moment, I knew which direction I was headed. I also knew that I would not be spending much time in the future with a guy who couldn't trust the zipper in at least one pair of pants.

Watched

"Okay," he said. "It's time to settle up."

Josh had that special look in his eyes and hadn't diverted his gaze elsewhere the entire evening. Anticipation, both nerve-wracking and exciting, filled Mindy's mind. Adrenalin flowed. His attention excited her, but he wouldn't propose again. She had made it known that her childhood bout of life-threatening rheumatic fever left her with severe health problems that she didn't wish on anyone.

They were huddled in a booth in the area's only vegetarian restaurant, a refurbished antiquated house on the edge of Walnut Grove in the Sacramento River Delta. The Delta is a sprawl of rivers, channels and canals that formed islands in a far-reaching portion of California's Sacramento and San Joaquin Valleys. The cafe was their favorite place to discuss the business matters of Mindy's small organic farm located on the two acres adjacent to her home on Grand Island.

Often times, groups of young people would visit her mini-farm to tour. Afterward, the group would relax on the back patio. She would lecture about the importance of growing their own food for better health. In particular, a couple of students, as she called them, had been coming since she began her talks. She treated them like family; family she no longer had because her few relatives died early, including her mom and dad. After managing her doctor bills all those years, her parents were left with nothing. An aunt that she stayed with afterward left her the small weathered farmhouse and land.

Relaxing over lunch, the ambiance of the cozy eatery attracted both those who managed their diets well and farmers who still used pesticides. Chattering happy voices drowned out soft music playing in the background. Ceiling fans wafted scents of spices and flavorings through the air and tantalized even the most reluctant to sample some new healthy fare.

"Settle up?" she asked. What was that about? Only halfway through the meal, surely, he couldn't be referring to the dinner bill. Plus, he would not allow her to pay, ever.

"Yes," he said, taking a sip of water as he studied her reaction. Finally, he said. "Ah, those exotic hazel eyes of yours!" He scooted even closer and ran a hand down the back of her hair and gently clutched a handful and studied it but remained quiet. She couldn't count the times he had complimented the way the sun bleached streaks in her auburn-brown hair while his hair had remained dark no matter how much time he spent outdoors.

She would often notice him watching her. His dark eyes exuded a sense of peace. He was kind, patient and understanding. "I wouldn't have guessed we were indebted to each other," she said, teasing. She laid her fork down momentarily. No need existed to rush through the meal to make way for other diners. She smiled and pushed gently against his shoulder. "Just stare out the window once in a while, okay? You make my heart flutter when I catch you staring at me."

Josh was friends with the owners who allowed them to use a booth set aside for management. Yet, the managers never sat, but mingled with the patrons helping them feel welcome. On one or two occasions, the owner joined them unannounced. His meal was placed in front of him without having to order. Mindy and Josh welcomed this kind of personal camaraderie.

"Things are heating up between us," Josh said, looking as if he couldn't stop smiling. When he had something serious to say, he would approach it in a jovial way. His smiling eyes were sure to develop crow's feet as he aged. Mindy had to smile. Suddenly, Josh frowned and looked serious. "I know why your rheumatic fever makes you shy away from me," he said. He was really trying to understand and she knew it, though at times he seemed obsessive about it.

If he was about to propose, she would decline again, perhaps not see as much of him, maybe stop seeing him, though the idea left her with an emptiness. Dealing with the bit of stress this caused put a strain on her weakened heart. How could she not see him? She loved him and that should be great for her emotions in a very healthy way. Yet, how could she dump her health malaise onto the very person whose relationship she cherished and wished to nurture?

His eyes held a look of knowing. He had already quietly laid his utensils on his plate and took her hands. "I just want you to know something," he said, taking a breath. "About me."

"As if I don't know a thing about you?" she asked. Suddenly she needed to break the tension. She smiled and crinkled up her nose. "So what are you going to tell me? That you're married? Or that you have a felony record?" She really was being facetious. She had checked his background scrupulously before he was hired.

He laughed, even bellowed. They had known each other nearly two years and just about bared their souls to one another. Except that she hadn't disclosed her deepest fears in order not to dump her garbage on him.

When they settled down, he asked, "Remember I told you about that load of pesticide that got dumped on me when I almost smothered to death?"

"That was, what? About five years ago?" It was her turn to be serious. "Oh Josh, it didn't make you permanently sick somehow, did it?" Pesticides were forbidden in Mindy's organic crops. It was one of the reasons that Josh vied for a position to work with her.

"No, nothing like that, but I just went through an extensive physical to be sure there could be no long term effects."

"So you're safe." She sighed, relieved that he was okay.

Before she could comment further, he said, "Safe, but I learned something else in the process. Listen. The docs did a whole work up on me. You know, like they do those soldiers that got hit with Agent Orange in Vietnam."

"And?" She was sure he was about to tell her the tests revealed something wrong with him. She could feel it in her bones and his expression confirmed it, but he had not served in Vietnam.

"Mindy, he said cautiously. "I just learned that I can't have kids."

She drew her chin back sharply. "Because of the pesticides?"

"Nope, that's something they happened to find, probably always been that way." He studied her face "That's all I wanted to say." His hand shook as he reached for his water. He eyed her over the rim of the glass. His stare was beginning to unnerve her. "Just a little quirk about me I thought you might find interesting," he said finally.

His information was most curious and lingered in her mind for days, especially while doing her favorite chore. She loved to sit in the sunlight getting a tan while pulling weeds in the yard. Her cardiologist said that if she proceeded slowly, it might be the best and only exercise in which she could participate; just sit restfully on the ground while enjoying doing the chore. Childhood rheumatic fever had so weakened her heart and inadvertently sapped most enjoyment out of her life.

Since their revealing dinner conversation, Mindy's mind filled with thoughts about why Josh would even mention his sterility. Without it ever being discussed, surely he figured out that she shied away from marriage for fear of becoming pregnant. The burden of carrying a child would put undue stress on her heart and cause it to fail, fatally, her doctor had warned, and most likely, long before the fetus could be saved. Her heart was just too weak. After that, her thoughts were that if she somehow managed to carry a child to term and herself passed away, that would leave the child without a mother. She didn't wish to bring a child into such a situation and that was her final thought.

Josh was probably on his way to Modesto. The year earlier, he had located the type of organic plant fertilizer they needed being used and sold at another farm farther south in the Central Valley. The bat guano made a huge difference in how her crops produced. It was less expensive for him to make the trip than to have it delivered. Mindy guessed Josh had planted the idea of how perfect she and he would be together and left her to think about it in his absence.

Josh would also stop by the small farms started by Yutu, a *Miwok* descendant from the tribes that once inhabited the Central Valleys. Yutu was one of her students. He struggled to hold onto the small patch of barren rocky acreage he had inherited. His tried to learn as much as possible, passing the knowledge to other Native American families in their destitute communities.

Mindy's weed pulling routine was to work at the edge of the rose bushes that bordered the fence. A few feet would be enough for one day. The yard itself had been planted with Dichondra that grew thick and cushiony, choked out stray weeds, and required minimal care. Tall old pear trees bordered the house and yard on three sides beyond the white picket fence. An old wide-trunked oak tree stood farther out; another on the neighboring property. The sun shone around her and a cool breeze blew in off the Sacramento River on the other side of the levee that fronted her property. She sat quietly at the edge of the lawn, enjoying the sunshine, with no thought of rushing to get started. If she didn't get much done, the field laborers also helped to keep the weeds down.

It was working in the dirt that caused her to start her own organic mini-farm, like so many residents in the Sacramento River Delta. She couldn't share in and enjoy the actual labor, which is why she hired a foreman to carry out her wishes. That was Josh Frohman, whose energy and commanding presence were the kind of strengths needed in the person to run the farm overall. A middle-aged woman named Helen Dewey, who had been laid off after thirty years on her bookkeeping job in Sacramento, was hired for the office help. Helen became a special friend and confidant. Mindy let her move into one of the bedrooms. Her presence was a comfort.

As Mindy sat with her few hand tools uprooting invaders around the shrubs, an enlightening experience overtook her, something she sensed trying to come to conscious thought. She had shied away from a committed relationship for fear of becoming pregnant. Why marry a man and not be able to give him children? She and Josh had not discussed this, but surely he had guessed her thoughts. That was the reason he told her he couldn't have children. He could not give her a child. Why had she not realized this immediately when he made his disclosure? The thought was stunning. She sat and stared straight ahead as a feeling of freedom washed over her. It was a burden lifted. Josh's attentiveness and caring had been unending. He loved her. He telling her he couldn't have children was a precursor to him proposing again.

Mindy smiled and shook her head. That was Josh's way of saying she would be safe with him. He meant to break it to her gently. Her mind flitted across the possibilities. They had so much life to live and it wouldn't be cut short. She started singing the Hawaiian wedding song: *I will love you longer... than foreve-r-rr...* At one time, when marriage seemed possible, she dared dream of a wedding in Hawaii, like a couple of her acquaintances had. Then came the bad news that she should not travel farther than into Walnut Grove or the small surrounding towns and certainly not fly anywhere. Still, her curiosity led her to research weddings in Hawaii on the Internet. A Hawaiian wedding could be arranged in the Delta, maybe on the beach at Steamboat Slough.

Friends admired her voice. At first she saw it as another opportunity missed, but realized early that her condition precluded much that gave others enjoyment. Still, she accepted her lot in life and got over it. She sat alone with the few employees tending their jobs at the other end of the field. Her elation carried her away. When she realized she was singing quite loud, she looked around to see if anyone had heard.

Out of the corner of her eye, she saw someone peeping out from behind the massive oak trunk. Watching. Her heart began to pound and that wasn't good.

She couldn't let that happen and pressed her hand against her chest and took slow deep breaths. Why would someone watch her? She looked again. The person must have ducked behind the tree. She hadn't seen him clearly. Maybe it was old Ray Beaner from the next property over. He might have been embarrassed at being caught listening. She smiled, knowing Ray Beaner often crossed the back of her property to chat with her laborers in the field. He must have heard her crooning. How embarrassing! The idea of being secretly watched and not understanding why the person hid continued to make her heart pound in anticipation of something unknown. That irritated her. She focused on the weeds under the rose bushes and pulled her sun hat down for more shade on her face.

So who was it? She was no dummy. Her body was fragile but she had a superior mind. She knew the workers liked her and were thankful for their jobs, but they remained reticent because of her condition. The thought that it might be a stranger crossing through the fields instead of following the winding levee and then hiding caused some fright and kept her pulse pounding. Somehow, she had to calm her heart rate. She rose as quickly as possible and made her way into the house.

As Mindy passed the doorway of the smaller bedroom-converted office, Helen, ever attentive, rose from the chair at her desk. "Mindy, back so soon?" Her expression turned serious. "You okay?"

"Too many people around," she said. She needed to lay down and rest. The thought of a stranger hiding and watching was unnerving. Mindy allowed Helen to help remove her shoes and stretch out on the bed. She tried to relax. "Someone was standing behind a tree watching me," she said. "I'm so embarrassed. I was singing too loud, I think."

Helen left the room and soon returned. "I didn't see anyone out there," she said. "But so what if someone heard you? One thing that rheumatic fever didn't hurt was your vocal chords."

* * *

Thankful for the truck's air conditioning system, Josh traveled from Walnut Grove to Modesto while the sun beat down and the mercury rose to triple digits. After picking up a load of fertilizer, he paused only to have lunch at a rest stop east of Modesto and give the truck a chance to cool down. He would deliver some of the guano to Yutu and couldn't wait to get closer to the Sierra foothills and cooler temperatures. He had been on the road too many hours and even thought about spending the night somewhere in the area and starting home before dawn when it was cooler.

Just as he climbed into his truck heading toward the foothills and wondering if he could crash with Yutu, his cell phone rang.

"Josh," Helen said, croaking into the phone. On that one word alone, her voice carried a ring of desperation. She was crying.

A shot of adrenalin raced through his nervous system, carrying a sense of dread. "Helen," he said. "What is it? What's wrong?"

"Come home," she said, barely choking out the words.

"What's happened, Helen?" he asked, screaming into the phone. "It is Mindy?"

Helen was crying too hard, all she could say was "Josh..." before the line went dead.

Josh sped home as fast as possible. His truck ran hot, bordering on overheating. Worry made him sweat in the air conditioned cab. He was thankful for the headset and tried several times to call Helen and could only leave messages. In frustration, he pounded a fist on the steering wheel, yelling at other vehicles and big rigs to get out of the way.

Josh yanked on the emergency brake and parked in front of the sign that identified *Mindy Moore's Mini-Farm*. He jumped the picket fence instead of unlatching the gate. As he burst into the house, all was quiet. "Helen?" he asked, calling out as he looked through the rooms. "Anybody?"

Helen came running in from the fields. "It's Mindy," she said, wringing her hands and sobbing as she collapsed into Josh's arms.

"Where is she?" he asked, his voice harsh and demanding. He helped Helen to sit and wasn't about to wait. He rushed to Mindy's bedroom and found it neat, like she always left it, though it looked as though someone had slept on top of the bedspread.

"Don't look," Helen said after regaining some composure. "Come sit down." She pointed and shook her hand toward the sofa beside her.

Josh knew it was bad news. Mindy was nowhere around. She must have been taken to the hospital, but Helen would have stayed with her. "Just tell me where she is," he said, begging. "I need to be with her."

Helen sucked back her tears. "Mindy's gone," she said. She starting weeping again.

"Get hold of yourself, woman!" Josh said. "Tell me where she is and I'll go."

"Gone, Josh," she said, her voice elevated. "Gone. She passed away."

Josh collapsed onto the sofa. He kept shaking his head and fidgeted nervously turning from one side to the other. He breathed heavily and clenched and unclenched his fists, trying to stave off the shock, not wanting to absorb the words that disbelief held at bay. He turned to Helen and grabbed her hands and began to cry. "Mindy? My Mindy's gone?"

"She's gone, Josh. She was so weak."

After hugging and crying, Josh had to build his resolve to get through the coming days. He swiped at his eyes. "Tell me what happened."

Helen retrieved a wad of tissues from her pocket, pulled a soggy one loose and blew her nose. "It was after you left to go to Modesto. Mindy went out to work in the yard. She hadn't been out but a few minutes when she came in saying too many people were around and she wasn't feeling well, said her heart was racing." She paused as Josh waited for the details. She blew her nose and continued. "Said there was a strange man crossing the back yard. Who would have known a simple thing like that could unnerve her? I got her to lay down on her bed and she seemed comfortable. When I went to check on her about an hour later… she was gone!" Helen couldn't hold back the new flood of tears. Josh wrapped his arms around her and together they rocked back and forth in sorrow.

Later, on the way to the funeral home, Josh called Yutu and told him he'd be several days late in making the delivery. He'd wait till he was there in person to break the devastating news.

A memorial service was held for Mindy right there in her yard around the goldfish pond she had installed years earlier. After she was cremated, her ashes were scattered in the flower beds under her beloved rose bushes.

Documented a year earlier when Josh and Mindy realized something special in their relationship, and when Mindy knew of his commitment to live organically, she had willed the house and farm to him through a trust. Josh both gladly and sadly accepted it in memory of the only woman he had loved.

* * *

The drive to the remote area of the Sierra Foothills was nothing but a vague memory. What he thought about mostly were the special times he and Mindy shared, and there were plenty. They had become nearly inseparable. He cherished it and his heart swelled, in spite of him coming to his senses and having to realize that she was gone forever.

The dusty rutted road from the highway to Yutu's farm a mile inside the border of the reservation jogged him back to his senses. Josh swung around and backed up toward the open carport which was used as a staging area for the farm. Yutu had managed to somewhat restore the old wind beaten deserted shanty. He was trying to set an example for the neighboring *Miwok* families, teaching that each could rise up out of squalor and build a new purposeful life. As a result, their houses were painted. Some modern conveniences had been added. Most importantly, the Miwoks sold their produce in fruit and vegetable stands along the highways and the meager earnings supported their improved lifestyles. He convinced some of them to give up drinking alcohol.

When the *Miwoks* began selling to the public, passers-by would stop, Yutu thought, just to see *what a real Indian looked like*. Yutu was a strong young man and his emotional presence among his people carried as much weight as Josh's presence did around the Delta. Yutu got over the insult and decided to make it work for him and his people. He was one of the first to let his straight black hair grow below shoulder length. He often times wore rooster and other tail feathers on a beaded headband. In the heat of the summer, he wore nothing more than a breechcloth hanging over a pair of shorts. His even brown skin accentuated the image he wished to portray.

He wore moccasins made by his people. When the curious wanted to buy some, Yutu began selling them and other handmade Native American artifacts at the roadside stands. As popularity for the authentic items grew, and more and more tourists began passing by, Yutu and his neighbors organized a Native American Festival. Children could ride mules and ponies. Adults could buy treasures made by hand. A few costumed squaws demonstrated how to weave wool and natural fibers into functional cloaks, hats and other specialty clothing. The food, of course, was the same the Miwoks themselves ate. Yutu credited Mindy for turning him on to some incredible possibilities. He absorbed every word that Mindy taught. He claimed she was the one person who did the most for his people; no one else, no government agency, only Mindy assuring him he was capable. Always emulating Mindy and her teachings, whenever he could, he talked to people about the *Miwoks* and how the tribes had lived throughout the Delta and Central Valley and how they had built many of the levees and canals still seen today.

Yutu came in from the field, rushing to meet Josh in the shade of the old carport. Yutu tried to shake hands enthusiastically. Josh could only hold tight. Yutu's radiant smile said he was happy to see his friend, but when he saw the look on Josh's face, his mood went somber. His arms dropped to his sides.

Josh didn't know how to begin. He had tears in his eyes. Surely his eyes were bloodshot from having cried in the truck when no one else was around to see him mourn. Yutu knew of Mindy's condition. Who didn't? How was Josh to tell that she had succumbed? As he drove, all he could think about were memories of their times together. He wished he had planned what he needed to say to break the news softly to Yutu. He could only stand still in shock and stare into Yutu's eyes.

Yutu began nodding. His eyes got glassy but he remained stoic. "Was it peaceful?" he asked.

Josh explained as much as he knew. Finally, they unloaded the bat guano. Yutu wanted Josh to go out into the fields. Josh saw it as diversion, though Mindy, in absentia, was nearly as much a part of this farm as her own.

Josh spent the night in Yutu's cabin. Neither spoke much, just sat on the porch for a long while and studied the stars, each needing to grieve silently. Once Yutu said, "When I find a girl like Mindy, I'll get married."

The long drive home the next day was an arduous trek back to a life and circumstance he didn't wish to live with. Again, his thoughts were only about Mindy, but he was cried out. Often he shook his head in disbelief.

One of the last cute things she had said to him was: *Just stare out the window once in a while, okay? You make my heart flutter when I catch you staring at me.* She was so cute when she teased.

He drove in silence, not remembering the road behind. As he neared the Delta, something began working its way into his consciousness out of the rush of memories. He remembered that he was supposed to leave for Modesto early in the morning to escape most of the midday heat, but he hadn't left and got a late start leaving. The workers had a problem with irrigation and he stayed to help. He had been crossing the field behind the house, rushing toward his truck when he heard Mindy singing. She seemed jubilant. He didn't want to destroy her mood so he didn't stop. He knew by the song she sang that she had finally understood the meaning of him telling her about his health issues. They couldn't be married in Hawaii, but they could now marry. When she wasn't looking, he slipped away. He would leave her to happily think about marriage plans till he returned that evening.

He was already feeling numb. It got worse. His thoughts still weren't clear. Helen said Mindy told her a strange man had crossed the back yard. So Mindy had seen him but didn't recognize him as he ducked behind a tree. Mindy had seen someone but didn't know it was him.

Again, her words played a mournful tune from memory: *You make my heart flutter when I catch you staring at me.* The memory of her playful voice tore at his emotions.

Josh gasped. He choked. He slammed on his brakes and skidded to the shoulder of the levee road. Mindy saw someone who hid and that unnerved her; unnerved her into having heart failure. It was him who ducked behind a tree, him not wanting to interrupt her moment of happiness.

He slowly pulled back onto the road feeling truly numb. After a long thoughtful and sorrowful drive, he parked in front of the sign, *Mindy Moore's Mini-Farm.* The site of it made tears gush. He choked again. He knew what he had to do and took a sharp, deep breath and held it while he pulled himself together. He needed to have a long talk with Helen. If he was the person responsible for Mindy's heart failure, he needed to own it.

The Swimmer

"You always appear out of a haze, like a beautiful figment of my imagination."

"Maybe that's what I am."

"Are you some sort of apparition?"

"I'm whatever you want me to be."

"Why do you swim alone in this dark, foggy lake?"

"I come to watch a troubled young man sitting alone under a tree, drinking."

"Come sit with me here on the bank. I brought cold beers."

"No, you must come to me."

"You seem like someone I could talk to. Why won't you come out?"

"Impossible. You must get into the water."

"I tried it twice and nearly drowned before someone pulled me out."

"Come into the water with me. That's why you've returned."

"Hey, I never see your clothes laying on the bank? Do you come here naked?"

"Clothes? Naked?"

"What's that you're floating on?"

"Oh, this?"

"What is that? Some kind of raft?"

"Not quite."

"I might go in if I had a raft to hold onto."

"It's not a raft."

"Then I won't go in."

"Too bad. I could solve your problem."

"Okay, come out for a while."

"I cannot."

"Why on earth not?"

"See this?"

"Your raft... a fish's tail?"

"It's not a raft, but it is a tail."

"A-a-r-rgh! Why did you splash me?"

"With my raft?"

"A tail? You're a... a... mermaid?"

"Yes!"

"I am losing my mind!"

"Yes."

"But... you're real."

"You created me, to help you get into the water again."

"To drown?"

"You'd have succeeded this time. Goodbye."

"Wait! I'm coming in... I'm coming...!

Thanatos

Every particle in creation carries the urge to return to its source, just as the wave that returns the sand to the shore retreats back into itself, the sea, to evaporate and rise to form the clouds, bantered by the winds, and even they retreat upon themselves and leave the clouds to rain down on the land and feed all blooming things that erupt through the crust from roots to bring up stems and leaves and buds that burst forth with flower and food, to feed every living thing in existence so they may grow and reach their full potential, before thanatos switches on the death instinct causing them to wither and die and be absorbed by the dust, as we in different forms of creation, nourish ourselves on various forms of that same life, brought by rains that cause streams and rivers to flow homeward to the sea, even though the ephemeral bodies we choose to inhabit incubates that same urge that will eventually return us to that source beyond creation by being planted in the ground or by the spreading of ash; ashes to ashes and dust to dust, not without reason of being, but first while living, to come to know that all things are a part of everything else, the great expanse, in inseparable bond, not just to know but to perceive with every cell of our being, that we are but a miniscule bit of creation, because we, unique and not at all unique but just another form of living thing, are made of the same elements and must finally understand that our every cell does not belong to us but to the everlasting unknown, like the life in the waves of the sea, the grains of sand, the wind, the plants of the earth, and even the earth's myriad inhabitants, and may extend far beyond earth to the nether regions of the universe, and far beyond that, too, like black holes that pull back in on themselves, all are created with the same urge; thanatos, keeps us in touch with the essence from which we are created, inborn and felt but unseen, an urge to be reunited with our Creator as our being silently pleads, carry me, carry me home!

Alien Footprints

A bloody heel print lay splattered on the floor near the wall, nowhere near the doorway. The toe of the shoe print was on the floor on the opposite side of the wall. It looked as if someone had walked there before the wall was set in place, but the house was old, the blood fresh.

"Somebody lured our victim into this abandoned structure," Police Officer Morrow said.

More prints led toward the opposite wall and disappeared with another heel print at the wall, as if the person had walked right through it to the outdoors.

Officer Morrow was stymied, but not quite. He was the only officer open to possibilities beyond the norm, especially when investigating homicides that included some strange elements and weren't quite normal. There were a few of them lately, in neighboring towns too. Such strangeness, like that shoe print. Too many weird crimes had happened in recent times. Officer Morrow was the only officer who dared think beyond the rational, especially when some events looked paranormal. He had also found a new recruit whose mother dabbled in tarot cards. Morrow could pick Kurt's mind about certain metaphysical phenomena. However, it was Morrow with his own sixth sense who was willing to look beyond the veil to find some answers.

"Outside," he said, motioning to Kurt. "Let see where these lead."

"But they stop at the outer wall," Kurt said.

Morrow gestured that Kurt follow along. They backtracked past the wall with the footprint half on one side, half on the other, and past the pool of blood and the mangled body on the floor that looked more like it had been slashed by an animal.

"Whoever or whatever it is that walks through walls," Morrow said, "can't hide its prints because the blood is human and humans don't walk through walls."

"But those are human shoe prints," Kurt said.

At the side of the house, the bloody footprints continued up and down the concrete walkway along the street, as if the person didn't know which way to go. The prints stopped near a window alcove. Many prints were there, as if a person had stood and bled. Morrow wasn't surprised. The way the body inside was slashed, it must have been a horrific fight. The assailant himself must have been hurt or completely saturated with the victim's blood.

As each bent in for a closer look, one of the footprints moved! Both of the officers jumped backwards. Morrow knew he was dealing with something that would be hard to explain, but witnessing along with Kurt. The footprints abruptly began to imprint on the sidewalk, quickly, like running away. Just footprints. They saw no one, just bloody footprints being laid down, one after another, with the speed of someone fleeing, and loose blood splattering in droplets. Each footprint left less and less blood.

"What the hell?" Kurt asked, sprinting off after the prints.

"Shoot it," Morrow said, ripping his own pistol from the holster.

"Shoot what?"

Morrow's gun jammed. "Shoot it, damn it!" Morrow said as they ran after the prints. "Shoot!" He was both screaming and terrified. He was nearly out of breath.

Kurt drew his gun. "What am I shooting at?"

"Just about where you'd want to hit a person," Morrow said. "Shoot, man! Before we can't see the prints anymore."

Kurt shot once. The footprints stopped, and then began again, slow, dragging. Kurt shot again and the footprints stopped. Both men crept toward whatever was hit but kept a safe distance since they saw absolutely nothing.

Slowly, a grotesque being began to materialize, curled in a fetal position on the sidewalk. It wasn't bleeding. Blood only showed on the bottom of its shoes and over its clothing, if what it wore was clothing. The shoes morphed into the most freakish clawed feet imaginable. As the head and face came into view, its eyes sunk into hollows like tunnels, with pin point rays of light shining out, though flickering as if losing power. The face began to morph into Morrow's wife's features.

Morrow jumped backwards. He understood right away. "You're not Calley," he said. "You're not my wife."

Suddenly the creature morphed into Kurt's dead brother. The weak attempt to replicate their loved ones was horrific. Momentarily, it morphed back into itself, a withered blue-gray being with those probing eyes and curved talons on the ends of four limbs. It wore a strange gray uniform fitting like a body glove and could well have been part of its skin. A blue-green fluid began to ooze out of the bullet holes and mixed with the soaking of the victim's blood. It ran off the cement walkway and into the gutter. The thing was certainly not from this world. Its torn uniform said it had certainly been in a fight. It tried to contain the loss of fluid by frantically pinching closed the bullet holes and other wounds. It whined a high pitched hum and stretched out the taloned end of a limb, as if asking for help. It kept pinching; the wounds kept spilling blue-green.

Slowly, the creature lost its struggle to stay alive and hissed like an animal as it decayed into dust and blew away.

Once the officers recovered their composure, Kurt asked, "How are we going to write this one up?"

No sooner did Kurt utter the words, the blue-green fluid on the concrete dried to a powdery substance and each particle erupted in a mini-explosion, hissing and popping till all the ooze disappeared, leaving only bloody footprints and drippings.

Morrow shook his head as he and Kurt stared at each other in disbelief. Morrow looked around. "Look there," he said, pointing to the human blood left from the creature that had dripped over the curb. "They'd say looks like whoever killed that guy inside the house there got clean away when he made it to his vehicle."

"DNA will prove this blood belongs to the victim. They'll believe someone else had to be horribly injured in that brawl that went on in there."

This crime sent Morrow's mind in a spin. "Yeah, yeah," he said, scratching his head. Something wasn't right. He felt suddenly horrified. "That thing tried to morph into my wife's features. Why did it try to become your brother too?"

Kurt shook his head. "He's dead. They never caught his killers either. Rumor had it that a gang of thugs took turns slashing him. He bled out."

Morrow was still deep in thought, putting the pieces together in the suspicious way that cops do. "It killed that man in there," he said. "You think that's what these... these aliens do in order to live.? They kill, but why?"

Kurt scratched his head. "Maybe they take over a body and live like that person. They could be infiltrating our world like that."

"Could be. It definitely ain't a vampire. This one didn't take blood," Morrow said. "It's all over the ground here and splattered inside the house. Maybe they take a person's life essence instead. Does that make sense?"

"Maybe these aliens, these creatures, snatch the soul," Kurt said. His eyes opened wide at the revelation. "After that, they morph into the person whose soul they stole and mix right in with us humans."

"But why try to become someone like your brother whose already dead?"

"If they're so smart," Kurt said. "Seems they'd just take over the body and kick the soul out into the ether someplace."

"This... this alien thing... he tried to morph into my wife first." Morrow looked straight into Kurt's eyes again and Kurt stared back. "Just call in the murder and wait for our guys," he said. "No report." Morrow was already heading toward the patrol car. "I need to go check on my wife."

Vibratory Rates

Heaven and hell are one, including purgatory and other holding stations in between. A friend told me one day that everything in creation, including us, is a vibration of energy. Different frequencies produce heaven and hell and all the rest right in the midst of what we call reality. When it's our turn to cross over is the moment we truly experience the fullness of being.

Our personal frequencies are connected with the beings that share our lives. When I pondered this, I surmised that though people pass from the physical realm, that meant their soul may still be around if we're each connected.

That might explain something else I pondered and was a little shaken by. As my friends passed away, before, during and after they die, I find myself thinking about other friends we'd known who have gone before. Strangely, I find little mementos they've left behind or which I connect with them. What we shared when each was here pops into my mind. Occasionally, when someone I know dies, I might think of someone I used to know, only to learn they had passed away long before. I also dream about the departed. So were these souls simply peeking through to send the message of their demise? Why would anyone come to mind as if they had just died? Why would these souls come back to visit coincidentally at the same time one of our vibratory kin passes?

If the universe and all else is energy vibration, one person leaving the body might open channels for departed souls to visit, like in sympathy as the death vibration revs its frequency to welcome another. One person crossing over opens a channel to pass through and the departed can attune to us, though briefly. A continuum until the people we once knew have switched frequencies. The friends who knew people we didn't know sort of keep the inevitable process going. Each new frequency of souls to cross over helps release those ahead from returning and helps push them toward a new destiny. I never knew my great grandparents and older ancestors. Maybe that's why they don't check in.

The Voodoo Kit

Jamaica was a wonderful vacation spot, except for the voodoo ceremony. I attended one and kept it secret from my disbelieving husband. Jim, an electronics wizard, had unexpectedly been invited to deliver a speech to an evening class at a local school. I found myself among strangers in a forest. After experiencing a live snake writhing around my neck, I vowed never again to dance myself into a trance. It's good finally being back in our country home, but something neither of us noticed at the airport was that someone else's suitcase was mistakenly switched for one of ours.

"Marla, I gotta run," Jim said after breakfast. "See what you can do about that case."

Getting our own suitcase returned could be a bureaucratic tangle in itself. I made numerous phones calls and learned was that no one had filed a missing luggage claim. The suitcase sits in the closet where Jim threw it. It should simply be returned to the airport.

When I went to retrieve it, a strange light showed under the closed closet door. When I opened the door, the light faded. The light showed again when I closed the door. I pulled the aging brown leather suitcase out and flopped it into a chair.

What was inside that case that seemed to glow? I opened the lid and barely held onto consciousness as the voodoo ceremony unfolded around me! I didn't lose consciousness this time and witnessed the full ceremony that I had missed the first time. The sound of the drums and the chanting seeped deep into me. Blood from the sacrificial chickens splattered over my face. A machete was flung! I ducked but heard a blood-curdling scream cut short behind me.

"This isn't happening!" The entry foyer began to fade away. I was being pulled back into the trance in the jungle again. I saw a tree and reached for the closest branch to steady myself. Several hands rubbed warm blood over me.

"Close it!" I said, hearing myself scream the words. Consciousness seemed fleeting but I managed to slam the lid and snap the lock. The chanting still rang in my ears, even as the blood faded from my body and clothing. My knees nearly gave way. I had to sit before I could stop shaking.

Why should the suitcase go back to the airport for someone else to fall under the spell when opening it? Had there really been a human sacrifice in the jungle? I saw the machete. I heard the scream cut short. Could this suitcase hold the evidence of a human sacrifice?

My mind reeled with questions but I couldn't rationalize what was happening. I couldn't return that voodoo kit. It was meant for me. I couldn't even tell Jim and have to disclose what I did in his absence. What had I brought down on us?

"I'll burn it," I said, eying the harbinger of evil. "Fire purifies."

The accumulated branches and leaves in the burn pit behind our house erupted into yellow, orange and red flames that licked ferociously toward the sky. I flung the suitcase. It sailed through the air landing on the heap of burning rubbish. My knees gave out but I had to watch and crawled on hands and knees away from the fire. Flames licked at the old leather. The drums, the muffled screams and crying seemed carried away on the flames. Fire would stop a hex.

Once back in the house, the shower was revitalizing. A good hot cup of coffee would be soothing.

Suddenly, Jim stormed in through the back door carrying the suitcase and the machete he used to cut the shrubbery. The suitcase had not burned!

"What are you trying to do?" he asked, as if he thought I had committed a mortal sin.

"It doesn't belong to anyone," I said.

Light showed from the suitcase. Jim followed my gaze downward. The light startled him. He dropped the case to the floor. The lid popped open and the voodoo scene reappeared as before, yet more powerful and entrancing than being in the jungle. A scream tore from my throat as Jim lunged at me with the machete.

Pekoe

A Port-A-Jon had been placed in the lot beside the Java Bean coffee house where I sat on the lanai fronting Kuhio Highway in *Kapaʻa*. The portable toilet should have been placed along the tree line behind the businesses. A new building was being constructed next door. As trade winds wafted carrying the smell, I couldn't imagine why the Jon was placed so close to the café's outdoor eating area.

Kilauea volcano wasn't spouting this morning. The *Halemaumau* Crater was on the Big Island of Hawaii at the south end of the Hawaiian chain opposite Kauai on the north. Each time Kilauea erupted, it sent volcanic ash into the air that stuck in the clouds and mists that the trade winds blew over the Islands. The *vog* painted the sunrises and sunsets pink, coral, and red. Mornings and evenings made for some spectacular photography.

I sipped my Chai and tipped my face upward enjoying the sun. Between the noises of passing cars, I heard faint mewing. A cat must have given birth to a litter back among the trees or under the building. A kitten was trying to get attention. As the mewing continued, I got up to learn where it originated.

I held my breath as I passed the Jon, but realized the mewing came from inside. I stared at that blue cubicle, putting my hand across my mouth and nose. Must I? I took a big gulp of fresh air and swung the door open. To my surprise, a teeny ball of orange fur lay on the floor. I grunted in surprise and expelled my breath. If not newly born, it had to be only a day or two old. It mewed and tried to move about but was much too young and still couldn't hold its eyes opened. When it tried to raise its head, it wobbled and fell back down. It was probably weak from starvation. A strand of shriveled umbilical cord was still attached. I gently but swiftly scooped it up, turned, and kicked the door closed with my heel. It was so tiny, it fit in the palm of my hand. On the way back to the lanai I checked and found the kitten was a male.

I sat on the lanai with this tiny sweet bundle on my lap. He had stopped crying and soon went to sleep in the valley between my thighs. I brought one leg up and propped my foot on another chair and kept my hand gently across his body to shelter him from the sun and wind. The owner of the Once More Consignment Shop, above the coffee house, saw the kitten and seemed truly surprised. "Where'd you get that little guy?" Lani asked.

"In the blue box," I said, nodding toward the Jon. "Someone abandoned him where he could be found."

Lani looked relieved but dashed off like she was on a mission. I sat there covering the kitten with my hand as the trade winds wafted over us. The gentle trades were fine with me, but this little guy could be cold. I drew the edge of my sarong over him and wondered how I might find him a home. He was so young, I wondered if he had ever been allowed to suckle. I didn't want to take him to the Humane Society. While those dedicated people would lovingly care for him, Kauai has so many abandoned cats that he might live in a cage for months or not given a chance to live.

I was about to leave when Lani dashed back with a handful of items. She had been to the Vet two blocks down and brought back a tiny bottle with a nipple and baby kitten formula. My heart went out to her selflessness.

"Can I feed him?" she asked. She must have fallen in love. She jumped up quickly saying, "Wait." She dashed upstairs to her consignment store and returned with an old soft tee shirt and wrapped the kitten in it. The kitten took the bottle immediately. "What'll we call him?" she asked. "Should we give him a Hawaiian name?"

"Not necessarily," I said. "He's the color of orange Pekoe tea. How about *Pekoe*?"

We giggled like young girls. Lani's instincts were more like a mom. Lani finally handed Pekoe back to me so she could tend to customers. Others on the lanai had crowded around to take a look. Everyone wanted to pet Pekoe on his head, which was the only thing that stuck out of the folds of the old tee shirt. I worried about that little knob being tapped on by so many and covered his head with my hand for protection.

Could I take this kitten home? My neighbor already has six large, prowling cats that hunted food in mine as well as the neighbors' yards. Those hungry animals kept the rats under control that came up from the nearby stream.

Fortunately for little Pekoe, the onlookers were enamored. None more so than Lani. She returned with a small cardboard box containing a cushion. "Are you taking him home?" she asked, sounding disappointed.

"I can't," I said. Lani's smile stretched across her face. I wanted to tell her about my neighbors' cats but she didn't give me a chance.

"I want him," she said, and that settled it. Pekoe would now—or when he was grown—be the mascot-guardian of the consignment shop. He would have his own rats to chase among the trees and underbrush in the back lot.

Lani, all smiles and giddy, carried Pekoe upstairs.

A bearded man sauntered over and sat down beside me. His clothes were clean, but stained from our iron-rich red dirt. "Where'd the kitty go?" he asked.

"Upstairs," I said, smiling.

"She gonna keep it?" He asked like he knew he was too late.

"Guess so," I said.

"I could o' used that cat," he said, standing and starting to leave. "Got a lot of creepy crawly things out on my farm." If Lani were forced to give up the store mascot, Pekoe would have another home waiting.

I scooted over into the shifted shade of the table umbrella and propped my feet on another chair. Heavy equipment sounds made me look. The Jon was being moved farther back. Kilauea wasn't erupting this morning and the trades blew fresh. I breathed in deeply as the nearby coconut trees swayed in the breeze. It was another magnificent day in paradise.

Great Lady of Wisdom

Some people eat goat.

On the property beyond the back yard fence where my neighbor Alana and I live in Hawaii, goats are raised and sold as food. Others use them in place of lawn mowers. Hungry little animals they are, eating and ruminating all day.

Alana had eaten goat meat when she was a child and thought it delicious. She has long since become a vegetarian.

Her leftovers get tossed to the goats. If fruits and vegetables in her refrigerator so much as droop or begin to wilt, it gets tossed to the hungry goats; a welcome change in diet from wild grasses and grain. They're like humans thrilling over an edible seldom included in everyday meals.

The goats love her food. The moment their gate is opened each morning, nearly all of them make a dash across the meadow, bleating and arriving at the downtrodden area opposite her side of the fence. They hurriedly find the goodies she's thrown out. I also throw out food. Alana's big thrill is hand feeding. Some of the goats rush right up to the fence in a smelly huff and accept the carrots, avocado peels, lettuce leaves and other delectable treats. Some try to climb the fence. Gluttons they can be.

Out of those diverse goats of different sizes, ages, colors and markings, Alana had a favorite. Her conversion to vegetarianism prompted spiritual renewal. She wears a golden Om meditation symbol on a chain around her neck.

"How can anyone eat such lovable animals?" she asked, sounding truly proud of her decision.

Yes, goats can be loveable, at least, these were. Temperamental goats can be friendly and cute. These look at us as if they understand the gibberish conversation Alana tries to have with them.

We became acquainted with personalities peculiar to each animal. One brown goat stayed back at the edge of the ravine seeming like a non-conformist, following and watching the herd. That nanny seldom came close in the beginning, but would watch. Alana enticed her closer by waving a sprig of broccoli in the air and throwing a piece in her direction. She was timid at first, darting away from where the broccoli landed.

One morning, Alana sat on her patio watching those ravenous creatures. The brown nanny happened by, the closest she had so far ventured. She was large and a subtle medium-brown, not a dirty black-brown or a brassy red-brown like some. Some black was present, down her spine to her tail and at her hooves, with a shadowy white arc across her head above her ears. The tops of her ears were also white, and in the middle of her forehead was a large round white mark.

"A *tikka* dot!" Alana said, excited to see such a mark on an animal.

Looking at her head-on, the lights and darks of her face symmetrically framed that dot. She surely was special. As if intentional, she turned, exhibiting her right side.

"Look at that!" Alana said, excited as her elevated voice carried over the fence to where I stood in my yard.

In the middle of the nanny's right ribs, from the top of her body to her underbelly and also in white, was a near-perfect reverse image of the Om meditation symbol Alana wore around her neck.

"A holy goat!" she said. How could such a marking appear on an animal, and reversed too?

The nanny ate near the fence in front of Alana for the longest time, as if inviting friendship. After a while, Alana retrieved her source book and paged to the section on female Indian names. That sweet animal with the reversed Om deserved a name.

I'd gone to the front yard and entered Alana's property through the side gate. I'm looking over her shoulder as she looks for names.

"That's a good one," she said. "*Mahesvari.* It translates to Great Lady." Since the Om, whether in frontal view or reversed represents the Sound of spiritual Wisdom, as Alana long ago explained, she searched for another name and found *Viveka.* That translated to Wisdom. So, with her limited ability to conjugate Indian names, she titled her four-legged friend, *Mahesvari Viveka,* which meant

Great Lady of Wisdom. At least, it meant that to the goat and to her and Alana knew they understood one another.

After that, every morning the great lady came with the group, running buoyantly with ears flopping like the others. "Just like me," Alana said. "Timid till I get to know you."

Maheshvari would eat the treats. Afterward, she'd stand without moving, staring intently at Alana through the dark, oblong pupils of her yellow goats' eyes.

Alana spoke softly to her day after day until the great lady knew her voice. Often times, she stood back by the edge of the ravine while the other goats relished the vegetables. She would come when called by name and jump against the mesh wire fence with her cloven hooves, trying to get closer to what might be offered. She became friendly enough that Alana was able to pet her. It made me wonder how anyone could eat a creature such as this.

Several weeks later, I noticed Alana standing out by the back fence with no goats present. The pasture was completely empty. Alana seemed in great distress. I rushed over to learn what might be wrong.

"The goats were sold," she said. Her eyes were red, her expression one of true sadness.

I wondered if the goats had been sold for use as pasture animals to keep the weeds down on someone's property, or if the whole herd had been sent for slaughter.

The Last Thing I Do

Passing of the clouds is barely perceptible, unless the boat rocks and disturbs their reflection before the water returns to glass. The landscape is completely calm, not a tree branch bending. Sunlight beats down, felt, and seems the only thing moving.

I sit endlessly, caught up in the serenity of the lake. I think long about the last thing that I must do, but haven't been out on the water since you left. Left, but not quite gone, and this is not the place. I will know when I find the spot, where you and I used to sit and pass the hours as precious time together waned.

I row. We used to take turns rowing. Our favorite pastime was to try to find the exact mid-point between opposite shores. I always had trouble locating the right spot but today I remember your words: *Just about where the church steeple on the hill comes into view.*

Your presence as always, with me, even after there is no bringing you back. You can no longer speak to me, but our playful bantering haunts my memories, as does our laughter.

I wait till the water has smoothed again. Then slowly, I open the urn and set you free from a mind that held you captive and kept us apart yet together for years; set you free to be the liberated soul that you are.

Future Winner

Kauai's heat and humidity were nearly unbearable due to the trade winds taking leave. The doors of the *Hale Hoʻokiʻiki* Gallery at *Kinipopo* Village in Kapaʻa on the laid-back east side stood wide open. I didn't wish to be the first one to arrive, but found others already there. I had time to meet some of the artists. Just in case, I carried a small portfolio of some of my other art.

My photography and one large floral oil painting were on display and for sale. I dared enter a contest for local artists and some of my work was accepted for the New Kauai Art expo of florals in canvas or photo. When I learned several weeks ago exactly what was accepted it made my heart pound. It seemed confirmation that I had chosen the right topics for my work. Taking a quick trip around the gallery rooms, I observed that at least one fourth of the artwork had sold tags attached but no tags graced any of my pieces. Also, as people circulated through the room, I noticed little interest in my displays. I felt a little unsure of my abilities at that point.

I stepped outside for some air. People milled about the small interior courtyard carrying drinks and 4pupus, *slices of Spam Musubi*, and chunks of grilled pineapple on skewers. A brown-skinned Hawaiian, in full native costume, sat whacking fresh cold coconuts with a machete. Cold coconut milk was a staple in the Islands. I recognized quite a few locals. On an island, those having something in common tend to congregate together. However, I saw some new faces too.

Chatting is not one of my strengths but I've learned to hold my own, somewhat. I greeted everyone I knew and was surprised at how many acquaintances were interested in art. Soon we were summoned back inside for the awards.

Awards ceremonies were something I enjoyed in the past and only wished my art could garner some accolades. Judges for this showing were well-known Kauai artists and gallery managers. One judge flew over from Honolulu for the occasion. Just my luck, too, that many of the artists in the show knew the judges. That made me nervous.

The presentation took a little too long and fans had to be brought in to circulate the air. Not all sold works won awards. Some unsold works won the best awards, pre-chosen before this day. My name wasn't called; no tag labeled any of my art as being sold or winning special recognition. I was deflated.

I wandered around the four small rooms and noticed the same people winning as usually did in most competitions. In fact, I was aware that some of the judges and artists were personal friends. I had to ask myself exactly what might be going on here. I sighed. I didn't know the judges personally, nor other artists either. I'm sure my shoulders must have sagged. Yet, I was determined to be a future winner.

The local newspaper photographer took shots of the winners. Attention was called to one person in particular who won "Best of Show." She had painted a scene titled "Beach Flowers." To me it looked more like sticks and stones in mud. Where was the glistening beach and frothy aqua-colored water at least bordered by morning glories and vines creeping around some lava rocks and across the sand? I was shocked as she appeared. She looked as if she had just walked in off the beach; stingy hair, old faded sarong, and rubber flip-flops on dirty calloused feet. I cringed. She must spend her days painting *en plein air* and neglecting day-to-day upkeep. The dull browns, yellows and blacks of the painting seemed to emulate the feel of her. I reminded myself not to be critical. She created something someone loved, regardless of my inability to interpret the work. My turn would come one day, but if I was supposed to get to know a few judges first, I'd find another way.

By this time, I was sorely disappointed in myself. I went to take one last look at my three-by-four foot painting of a red hibiscus that I titled *Big Red*, hanging in a gallery, for this short duration anyway. It offered a spectacular burst of color. Viewers may remember it as not having won a thing. I wish I could have snapped a photo of my canvas hanging in a show for the first time but pictures were not allowed, not even by the artists themselves.

As I made my way through the crowd, I was surprised to see a middle-aged woman wearing a tasteful Hawaiian dress and a distinguished-looking man with gray hair and wearing white shorts and an expensive *Tori Richards* aloha shirt viewing my hibiscus. They nodded and smiled but hadn't taken their eyes off the canvas. They stepped back to see it in total, then stepped forward again to examine it close up. My heart began to pound. I slipped closer, pretending to examine the next painting over.

"Isn't this wonderful?" the woman asked with a New York accent as I sidled in.

"You like *Big Red*?" I asked.

"We wish to see more of this artist's work," she said. "We could use some big exquisite canvasses. This artist has a knack for great angles in her macro photos too." She gestured around the room.

My antennae went up. My heart leaped up into my throat. "I think that can be arranged," I said, bringing up my portfolio.

"Do you work here?" the man asked.

I was so tickled I couldn't stop my teasing smile. "This is my painting," I said.

Surprised, the woman gestured to what I carried. She asked to see my portfolio. Her gleaming gold *Kuuipo* and other *Hawaiian Heirloom* bracelets jangled as she quietly flipped through the clear plastic encased pages. Seeing a desk near the doorway, she sat down to peruse them more thoroughly.

Her husband looked over her shoulder. "Ah...!" he said. "Ah!"

"Yes, this one... and this one," she said, flipping through pages.

My emotions careened up and down. In a room full of people, no one came to interrupt. Had they sensed something important happening for me?

The woman stood and offered her jeweled hand. "I'm Eve Hutton," she said. "This is my husband, Benny." She caught her breath and asked, "Where can we see the rest of your work?"

Shaking hands gave me enough time to compose my thoughts. I didn't want to seem too eager. "Are you new in town?" I asked, hoping this distinguished couple wouldn't think I was new to the shows.

"We are," Benny said. He produced a business card and pulled several eye-catching brochures from his shirt pocket.

I looked at them briefly and, inwardly, had the biggest Aha! moment of my fledgling artist's career. Benny and Eve were owners of the soon-to-be-opened *Ma'alea Gallery* in Poipu on the island's upscale south shore.

"We've moved to Kauai," Eve said. "Retired and closed our gallery in New York and relocated to paradise."

"Art is our lives," Benny said. He smiled warmly. "Evidently yours too."

"Art in all its forms," I said. I was so beside myself.

"In that case," Eve said. "We've decided we like your macros too. No one here has done macros that come close to what you've produced. Your gigantic Big Red painting is spectacular." Her hand swept across the portfolio. "This orange slate pencil urchin photo is extraordinary."

"The urchin is from my underwater collection," I said, unable to stop smiling.

"So when can we see more of your art?" Benny asked again. "We're planning a grand opening titled *Future of the Arts*. We could use some *giclees* too."

I advised them that my studio is one bedroom in my simple island home, with my walls covered in art. As to some large *giclees*, pictures of their choosing could be ordered from my online gallery, custom framed and matted to their specifications, and received in plenty of time before their opening.

Eve, in turn, told me they so loved my art pieces that they would place me in the best room in their gallery. My gigantic eye-catching red hibiscus would receive some spectacular lighting. They had not asked anyone else at this showing to join in but had already signed up three other artists from around the island. These wonderful art lovers picked me out of this group!

"Four artists is the max we'll take at one time," Benny said.

I'm sure they've looked at other galleries and showings around the island if they've already chosen three others, but they picked me from this showing. An expo with other selected artists didn't intimidate me. It was a fantastic compliment. Eve had just said they would give my pieces the best room in the house. My art would appear on their brochures and in the local newspaper, along with the other artists too.

So what if I didn't win anything or make a sale today. Something serendipitous and grand has happened for me. I hope that when Eve and Benny Hutton come to my home, they will consider the four-by-four foot work in progress of a pink and yellow Rainbow Plumeria cluster that I've almost finished.

Innocence

Elise and Joe broke up. She was a senior and Joe was already three years out of high school. He flirted with me when attending school functions with Elise. The slow way he secretly winked at me made me think he liked me more than her. Classmates saw us flirt too. Some of the girls wondered why he went with Elise when I was much prettier. I didn't know about that. My friends say he dated her because she puts out. He also dated Shera and Clarissa. The kids in school gossiped, saying that those two put out to anyone, but they weren't the only girls Joe was said to be dating.

I stayed away from the talk. My best friend, Cindi, and I decided it was just a lot of idiocy. Joe was every girl's dream. When Elise and Joe broke up, I saw my chance. Joe and I have secretly seeing each other the past three weekends, Friday and Saturday evenings. "I've been deeply attracted to you," he told me when we first got together.

I had to ask. "Did you do it with Elise?"

He curled up the corner of his mouth and rolled his eyes, like he was embarrassed. "Nah, we never got that close."

"But you dated for two years."

"I guess she wanted to move on." He looked at me curiously. "It wasn't serious. I date a lot of girls." His smile widened. "You could be my only girl, if you wanted."

Somehow, I think he only mentioned his dating others to make me jealous.

Ten o'clock was curfew set by my mom and dad. I met Joe again when I left Cindi's house early one evening pretending to want to walk home. In the darkened school yard, Joe pressed hard against me till the back of my hips hurt against the concrete wall.

"Let me!" he said, pleading. "You know you want it too." His hot breath swirled across my neck.

I wanted to lay down right there in the shadows on the school lawn and let him have me, but why hadn't he tried to kiss me? If a guy cared, wasn't the kiss what came first? This was happening too fast, and not the way I thought it should. I tried to kiss him and rub my tongue against his lips like I heard other girls talk about, but he pulled away fast. Wasn't it a kiss that would start it all?

He wrapped his arms all the way around my waist till it seemed we'd melted together. Feeling his excitement between us, I almost gave in. "I can't, Joe. Not like this." I was just as aroused. He knew it too, but why hadn't he tried to kiss me. I really wanted to feel what it was like to be kissed the way I heard about.

Clouds in the sky broke apart. The position of the full moon up there shocked me to my senses. I glanced over Joe's shoulder at my wristwatch. It was five minutes till curfew. If something was to happen to bring Joe and me together, it wasn't going to be tonight.

I pulled away abruptly. Joe looked hot and shook up and a little dazed. "Fuckin' curfew!" he said under his breath.

"If I don't get home, Mom and Dad will put me on probation for a month." I ran the three blocks from the school yard to our house.

Mom and Dad sat in the living room playfully feeding each other popcorn and watching an old movie. That's what I wanted; the comfort of a loving life partner, although what we might feed each other wouldn't be popcorn.

Mom saw me. "You're such a good girl," she said. "Always home on time."

Little did she know that I could have the boyfriend of my dreams if I could have stayed out longer. He'll be mine soon if I can get past being scared about doing it the first time.

I thought Cindi knew about me and Joe, but how could she? He and I saw each other secretly. I wasn't ready to tell anyone that me and Joe were going together till I was sure of him. If we went all the way, he'd be mine. After that, I could let everyone know. Still, I was so happy that I wanted to share my secret with my best friend.

Monday morning at school, I walked in to find everyone talking excitedly in the hallway. Some of the girls with the big bad reputations stood crying, which was strange because they usually acted tough. The guys and girls stood apart, which was unusual too. The guys looked confused. I didn't hear Elise's showy voice and personality, which usually dominated the halls. Shera, nearly weeping, grabbed Clarissa when she came through the doorway and told her something that made her turn white as a ghost and faint dead away, right there in front of the book lockers.

I found Cindi and asked, "What's going on?"

"You haven't heard?"

"I just got here."

"It's Elise. She's gonna die!"

"Wha-at?"

"You know that guy Joe, don't you? The one she's been dating?"

"What about Joe?" I asked.

"He gave Elise HIV!"

Sister Fly

My sister killed a fly. Everyone in our family agreed on how she would reincarnate.

Homeless, Not Heartless

A homeless man, acting like a wounded lion expelled from the pride, foraged in a dumpster behind a restaurant. He looked like he hadn't eaten in a year.

"Gotta eat," he said, muttering. "Gotta eat."

He piled up remnants of discarded burgers on a piece of cardboard. He sampled one patty, then laid it down.

"Good, that's fresh," he said.

He found some chicken bones and other leavings.

The man seemed excited and sat down and neatly arranged the food, as if preparing to feast. Instead, he whistled, short and shrill, and his dog came running for its meal.

Roots

I was researching our family tree. We are upstanding people and I wondered from what kind of stock we originated. What I found was a lot of broken branches that should be pruned, or, at least, left to grow unnoticed and wither on their own. As I dug deeper, I discovered the worst yet. Root rot.

* * *

Publication Credits

A few stories in this collection appeared or were reprinted in the following publications.

Flash! Journal Anthology
The Shine Journal
Silver Boomer Books
Harauh - Breath of Heaven
Moondance International Film Festival Newsletter
Mississippi Crow magazine
Authorlink
The Voice
Changing Courses
Generation X International Journal
Seasoned Greetings
Gator Springs Gazette
Mountain Luminary
Five Star Productions, Inc.
Webstatic
Moondance ezine
It's All Happening at the Zoo
Hinduism Today

About the Author

Writing has been an interest since I was a child. Many of the scribbles and bits of profound thoughts that I committed to paper when younger remain on paper. Some of the ink has bled out into the page making many of the words nearly illegible. Nothing may be done with these notes except to affirm that writing has always been an interest.

In the late 1960s while I lived in San Juan, Puerto Rico, I thought I would write a few short stories. Then I thought I'd like to write a novel. One such novel was started but remains unfinished. I had to rush home to San Francisco due to an illness in the family. It was a permanent relocation for me. With the new life came new responsibilities and, unintentionally, writing was put aside. Now, among all the other stories I'm writing, I am revisiting that novel. That would be a huge undertaking. That story sits on the back burner with many other projects. Yet now, decades later, my muse has begun kicking out scenes and lines of dialogue that can only fit that story.

In the 1970s I wrote for and helped publish a monthly newsletter. From that time on, writing began to come to the fore, little by little. In the 1980s, after much experience, I published my own monthly newsletter and began writing poetry and short stories.

Not until being rear-ended in a car accident in 1991 did I begin to seriously think about publishing anything. Physical therapy lasted nearly three years and left me with nothing to do but think. I decided if my body didn't work well, my mind still cooked. From shortly after the accident, sitting still at my computer didn't cause my body to ache; it only hurt when I moved about. I sat. I conjured stories. I wrote.

My first novel was a whopping 134,000 words and immensely cathartic, not to mention being great experience at finishing such a monumental task. That book has not been published. In fact, I used some of the detail to include in

River Bones, my third published novel. However, now, twenty-seven years later and much writing since, I am rewriting that first story. It could use a lot more cutting to bring the word count to saleable size, but at least I have a lot of material from which to choose.

A native of Walnut Grove in California's Sacramento River Delta, Mary Deal has also lived in the Caribbean, England, the Hawaiian Islands, and presently makes her home in Scottsdale, Arizona.

Find Her Online

Her Website: http://www.marydeal.com
Amazon Author Page: http://tinyurl.com/3z8pm31
Barnes & Noble: http://tinyurl.com/o7keqf7
FaceBook: http://www.facebook.com/mdeal
Twitter: http://twitter.com/Mary_Deal
Linked In: http://www.linkedin.com/in/marydeal
Google+: http://tinyurl.com/pee51xz
Goodreads: https://www.goodreads.com/MaryDeal
Cold Coffee Cafe: http://coldcoffeecafe.com/profile/MaryDeal
BookTown: http://booktown.ning.com/profile/MaryDeal
Authorsdb: http://tinyurl.com/nnbk7lo

Her Art Galleries

Mary Deal Fine Art
http://www.marydealfineart.com
Island Image Gallery
http://www.islandimagegallery.com
Mary Deal Fine Art and Photography
https://www.facebook.com/MDealArt
LocalMe
http://www.redbubble.com/people/localme
Pinterest
https://www.pinterest.com/1deal

Lightning Source UK Ltd.
Milton Keynes UK
UKHW041842151020
371670UK00007B/112